"They think it's too easy...

At break, I finally saw it – well, one of them. A notice taped to the wall just outside our classroom said, in straggly black felt tip, RACHEL KELLY IS A SLAG. SHE'S SLEPT WITH THE FOLLOWING BOYS. A list of boys' names followed. It included Sim, Lloyd, Paul and even mentioned the school caretaker, Mr Barlow.

I ripped it down, my face flaming. But there was another, larger one outside the gym, featuring a caricature of me wearing stockings, suspenders and a bra. An even worse one was outside the boys' toilets. CALL RACHEL FOR A GOOD TIME, it proclaimed, and then gave my phone number.

I was devastated. All I wanted to do was hide away from the human race. I raced off to the loo, locked myself into a cubicle and burst into tears.

Other books also available in this series:

Look out for:

"They think I'm too easy..."

Lorna Read

SCHOLASTIC

Scholastic Children's Books
Commonwealth House, 1–19 New Oxford Street,
London WC1A 1NU, UK
A division of Scholastic Ltd
London ~ New York ~ Toronto ~ Sydney ~ Auckland

First published in the UK by Scholastic Ltd, 1998

Copyright © Lorna Read, 1998

ISBN 0 590 11156 6

Typeset by Falcon Oast Graphic Art
Printed by Cox and Wyman Ltd, Reading, Berks.

10 9 8 7 6 5 4 3 2 1

Prologue

Looking back on it all now, I think that if Mum had had more time for me and Carol-Ann hadn't gone off to art school, I mightn't have got myself into such a mess. Mind you, I can't blame other people for the fact that I'm a bad judge of character.

What a total dork I was to think Sim really loved me! And how could I have chosen Lori as a best friend? It seemed we had a lot in common. We always had great giggles together at school. But there was one big difference between us: she had a steady boyfriend, Carl, and I didn't, so she felt superior. And when I did start going out with boys and enjoying myself, she got jealous because she didn't have the guts to leave boring Carl, and she was just looking for some reason to pick on me. That's how Carol-

1

Ann, my big sister, explained it, anyway, and I think she's right.

Trouble is, the truth of the present is never revealed until it's already in the past. And if that sounds obscure, then blame it on my brain, which I wish I could trade in for a transplant!

The other thing I can't blame other people for is the fact that I slept around. It was completely my decision – though nobody would ever believe the truth, that all I was really doing was trying to wipe out Sim's memory and get my self-confidence back. I know I'll never get Gary to believe it.

I don't know if I'll ever see Gary again now, and the thought is tearing me apart. I love Gary. I more than love him if such a thing is possible. And I've thrown away my chances with him because I threw away my body – on Sim, on Paul, and on Lloyd. If only I could have the last nine months over again, I'd live them so differently. I'd be as pure as the driven snow.

Sometimes, I wish I hadn't had to grow up. Then I wouldn't have needed to know anything about S-E-X. But I *did* need to know, and there was nobody to ask. There were magazines, but they're not the same. They never write about your exact problem. They tell you about how to use condoms and how to have orgasms, but they don't tell you what happens afterwards – that boys can be rotten bastards and let you down, just when you've fallen in love with them.

But it's too late for all that now. Now I've got big problems – really mega enormous ones. Ones I'm going to have to sort out for myself. And it all started the day I first spoke to Sim. . .

Chapter 1

I'd never really thought about Sim until Lori started teasing me about him. She'd been my best friend for about a year, ever since Janice, my previous one, had gone abroad with her parents.

"I think Sim fancies you," Lori said. "He's always hanging around staring at you. Look — there he is now, over there by the railings."

I'd seen Sim around, of course. You could hardly miss him. He was very good-looking and he always seemed to have girls talking to him. The reason I'd never thought about him was because he wasn't in our class, and you know what it's like — people in other classes hardly exist unless you happen to be going out with them. I'd gone out with a few boys, but only for a couple of dates each. They'd never fallen in love with me and wanted me to go steady, so in my opinion I was a total romantic failure.

I blamed it on the fact that I can be a bit quiet and timid, and have awful brown, frizzy hair which I hate. Carol-Ann, my sister, has wonderful smooth blonde hair. Life isn't fair! All the blokes I know treat me like a mate, so whenever boys tried to chat me up, I teased them and joked with them, like I would with my brothers.

I'd been told by snidey Rosie Francks, my worst enemy, that I gave boys the wrong impression and acted as if I was throwing myself at them. "Rachel's giving herself a bad reputation. She should learn to act cool instead of being so overfamiliar," she told Lori, who told me. But who cared what Rosie said? She was a cow and nobody liked her except Shaz and Barbie, the other members of the Gang of Three, as we called Rosie & Co.

"You're joking, Lori. You must have got it wrong," I said.

"No, I haven't. Look, look!" She nudged me excitedly, her brown ponytail swinging.

I turned my eyes in the direction she was pointing. Sure enough, Sim was staring our way.

"It must be you he fancies, not me," I said. "Boys never fancy me." Though I was thinking:

given half a chance, one word of encouragement, I'd go out with him like a shot! He was simply gorgeous.

"It can't be me. The whole school knows me and Carl are an item," she said. It was true. They'd been going out for two whole years.

"Why don't you just kind of wander past him and see if he says anything? Go on, Rachel, I dare you," she said.

"I can't!" I protested. But I did. I pretended I was going to talk to Donna. I needed to, actually, as she'd borrowed a tape off me and hadn't returned it yet, and it just so happened she was standing in a very convenient place, just past where Sim was.

As I got near him, I started to feel all wobbly and nervous. I tried not to look at him but my face was burning and I felt sure I was about to trip over or do something equally stupid. He'd stopped looking at me and was staring at a book instead. Then, just as I thought I'd got safely past him, I felt a hand on my arm and jumped out of my skin.

"Hey," Sim said. "Not so fast."

"What do you mean?" I asked him, feeling the heat of embarrassment flare in my face again.

"I mean, you're always dashing past me. Why not stop for a chat sometimes?"

I stared at him, noticing for the first time that he had silvery grey eyes. I'd never seen anyone with eyes that colour before.

"Why should I? I don't know you," I said.

"Of course you do," he told me. "We've been at the same school for years."

"I know that, but we've never talked," I pointed out.

"Then let's talk now. I'd like to get to know you, Rachel," he said.

I shot a wild glance across the yard, to where Lori was standing, gazing at us. I could tell she was hopping with curiosity. She gave me a thumbs-up sign.

"How do you know my name?" I asked him.

He tapped the side of his nose. "Sleuthing," he said mysteriously, and wouldn't tell me any more.

"So . . . what would you like to know?" I was starting to enjoy myself.

"Everything. Where you live, what your interests are and whether you've got a boyfriend or not." He smiled again and I felt all warm and wobbly once more.

Then I pulled myself together, pinned on a grin and looked him straight in those silvery eyes. "The answer to the last question is no, not at the moment. I'm footloose and fancy-free," I said boldly.

7

"Then will you come out with me? How about a pizza tomorrow?" he invited. "You can answer all my other questions then."

Privately, I thought that wouldn't take long. I didn't have many interests at all and I felt sure he'd get utterly bored and walk out on me before the date was over, but I still accepted his offer of a date. Who wouldn't?

I tried to act cool when I got back to Lori, but she got it all out of me and made me promise to tell her everything. Later, I wished I hadn't made that promise. Once you start the truth game, it can become a habit you can't break. It gets like a form of blackmail. That's what happened between Lori and me.

My first date with Sim! How I wished Carol-Ann had been there so I could tell her about it, but she'd left home a year ago to go to art college in London. I tried ringing her at her flat but a woman answered and said she was out and she didn't know when she'd be back as she hadn't seen her for a few days.

Carol-Ann isn't my only sister. I've got Joanna, too, commonly known as Jo-Jo. No point telling her about my love life, though, as she's only two and a half. I've also got three brothers – Jamie, Jo-Jo's twin, and two older ones, Ollie and Pete.

I was the baby of the family till Jamie and Jo-Jo came along. They were the last straw for Mum and Dad's marriage. Just as they thought they were going to have some time to themselves at last, Mum fell pregnant at forty-one and Dad waltzed off with a young girl from the office.

We've hardly seen him since. Mum wouldn't have him in the house and Dad now lives hundreds of miles away in Aberdeen.

To make ends meet, Mum had to park the babies with a child-minder and get a full-time job in a boring insurance office, as my two spoilt slobs of older brothers were both on the dole and showed no signs of either getting jobs or pulling their weight around the house.

I'd long ago given up even trying to confide in Mum. She was always too busy or too tired. If I told her I wanted to talk to her, all I got was a vague, "Not now, dear. Later." So I did all my talking to Lori, and sometimes to Mary and Kirsty, two really nice girls from my class. If they didn't have each other as best friends, I felt sure I'd have been best friends with one of them.

So now you know why I didn't tell Mum about my first date with Sim. I just got ready and prepared to slide out of the house without anybody knowing. But I hadn't reckoned on bumping into Mum coming up the stairs.

"Mmm, you smell nice. That smell's a bit familiar, though. It's not my new perfume, is it?" Mum remarked as I wafted past her.

"Sorry. You left it lying around the bathroom so I borrowed some. You don't mind, do you?" I asked guiltily.

"Not so long as you don't make a habit of it," she said. "Are you going out tonight, then?"

"Yes." I paused. "I've got a—" But before I could get out the word "date", there was a loud crash from the twins' room, followed by a wail, and Mum had to go dashing off, which gave me time to sneak into her bedroom and borrow a dab of her amazing mascara which transforms stubby lashes into spiders' legs.

I met Sim outside the pizza restaurant. He was looking really cool, in black 501 jeans and a black padded leather jacket, and a dark green T-shirt.

"Hi, Rachel! You're looking nice," he said approvingly.

I had made a great effort to minimize my bodily imperfections. I was wearing a tight black stretchy top and my black jeans were a smaller, female version of his own. I had a black leather jacket on, too. We must have a lot in common if we wear such similar clothes, I thought.

I admired the masterful way in which he asked

the waiter for a quiet table for two in the no-smoking section. So he didn't smoke; that was another thing in his favour. Far too many of the boys in our school did. *And* the girls. I'd never tried it. I had to breathe enough smoke at home, with Ollie and his mates puffing away and polluting the atmosphere. The poor twins' lungs didn't stand a chance.

The waiter asked if we'd like a drink and we both said "Coke, please," at exactly the same moment and burst out laughing. It broke the ice and in no time we were discussing whether we preferred pizza or pasta, what kind of toppings we liked, and we'd soon got on to other topics – brothers and sisters (he had two sisters, called Mandy and Mel), school, the teachers, holidays.

He made me laugh by telling me things he and his sisters had got up to when they were kids. I did most of the listening, but I didn't mind because he was being so entertaining.

I hardly noticed how the food tasted, I was so absorbed in Sim's anecdotes. I had expected to be really nervous, but I wasn't. Not, that is, until he suddenly put his hand out and got hold of mine as it rested on the tabletop. I went rigid and stopped breathing, aware that he was gazing deep into my eyes.

"I really like you, Rachel," he said. "I just wanted you to know that."

I suddenly lost all appetite for the ice-cream dessert I'd ordered, but as he'd insisted this meal was to be his treat, I forced down a few mouthfuls.

After paying the bill, he escorted me out into the damp, chilly November night. It was only twenty-five to ten.

"Where would you like to go now?" he asked me.

I'd sort of assumed I'd be going straight home, so I didn't have an instant answer.

He took my silence as meaning I had no suggestions, so he came up with a few of his own. "Would you like to go for a drink? Or we could go to a club. . ."

"I'm not dressed for clubbing," I replied.

"A walk, then."

It was really cold, but in the end that's what I agreed to.

A canal runs through our town. Once, it had carried horse-drawn barges full of slate from the mines. We'd been given a talk about it at school; that was how I knew. Now, it had been prettified with newly painted lamp-posts and hanging baskets of flowers in the summer. There were one or two canalside restaurants and pubs which, in good weather, put out tables and chairs over-looking the water.

We took one of the narrow lanes between rows of old workmen's cottages, and walked either side of a metal bollard which prevented cars from parking at the canalside. There was a cold, steely light on the water, the surface of which was ruffled and tufted by the wind. The bunches of whipped-up water looked as solid and black as the metal of the bollard we'd just passed.

I shivered and wrapped my scarf more tightly round my neck.

"Cold?" said Sim.

"Uh-huh," I admitted.

"Come here," he said.

He put his arm round my waist and pulled me to him, so we were walking hip to hip, our leather jackets creaking together. We were out of step with one another. With each stride, our flanks bumped uncomfortably, so I gave a little hop so that our steps matched.

His hand reached for mine. I had a woolly glove on, but he was bare-handed and he must have felt the cold, because he clutched my hand and shoved his and mine into my jacket pocket.

A duck quacked loudly on the water and we stopped to look.

"Do you think ducks feel the cold?" I asked Sim.

"Not them, they're floating duck-down duvets!" he laughed.

I had a sudden mental image of being under a feather duvet with Sim. It made me shiver.

"You *are* cold, aren't you?" he said. He turned me round to face him and wrapped both arms round me so that I was fastened tightly against him. Not in a million years would I have confessed that I now felt boiling hot!

I felt his breath against my forehead as he bent his head.

"Rachel," he murmured, "can I kiss you?"

I couldn't reply. My vocal cords were completely paralysed. It was all I could do to remember to keep on breathing.

He was crushing me in his arms. I was on tiptoe, my mouth pressed against his. His tongue was flickering to the left, to the right, then its wet, pointy tip was trying to wiggle its way between my lips. I resisted for as long as I could, then I let my mouth relax.

I'd never admitted to any of my friends, apart from Lori, that I'd never French-kissed a boy. Most of them had gone far, far further than that. I would have looked a real fool if I'd said I'd never even had a proper kiss. But I hadn't. This was it!

The dark, windy night sky swirled around my head. I could feel and hear the stars and the wind swishing in my brain. I was dizzy and weak from holding my breath as I didn't want to breathe into Sim's mouth in case I tasted of onions.

Then, suddenly, I forgot all my worries as something happened, something clicked into place, and the kissing took me over.

Chapter 2

Next day, Friday, Lori was waiting for me outside school, desperate to hear my news. When I
told her about our long, smoochy kiss, she closed
her eyes and sighed.

"I wish Carl would kiss me like that," she said.
"He used to, right at the beginning, but now he
hardly bothers with kissing."

I didn't like to ask her what he bothered with
instead. I just smiled absently, reliving that
kissing session.

"When are you seeing him again?" Lori
asked.

"I don't know," I told her. He'd taken me
home, kissed me again on the doorstep, then
walked off, saying he'd see me in school next
day.

"Well, let me know what happens," she said. "I don't get any excitement in my life these days. Carl's so predictable."

"Well, I'm not going to say what I always say," I promised her, meaning that she should finish with Carl. We both knew she never would. He was great-looking, came from a well-off family and was all set to follow his dad into the family business. If she'd wanted to pick good, safe husband material, Lori couldn't have done better. They were even talking about getting engaged on her eighteenth birthday.

I didn't have long to wait for the next instalment of my own personal romance. I dreamed my way through the morning's classes and was just standing in the corridor, taking my sandwiches out of my bag, when I heard a voice saying, "Hello, Rachel!" and there was Sim walking towards me.

I nearly fell over. My plastic sandwich bag dropped from my paralysed fingers and Sim picked it up for me. "Mmm, cheese and lettuce," he said. "You weren't really going to *eat* those, were you?"

"Well, I *was*. . ." I said, feeling faint as I gazed into his eyes. It was as if he were putting a spell on me. I felt that, if he beckoned his finger, my feet would go sliding across the floor towards him, as if he had me on an invisible string.

"I was looking for you to ask if you'd like to come to Casa Gut-rot."

Its real name was Casa Mia and it was the local greasy spoon, situated by the entrance to the park. It served cheap meals of egg and chips, mushy peas, and burgers that could have swum the Channel, they were coated in so much fat.

I pulled a face.

Sim took it the wrong way. "Oh. So you've got other plans, have you? I'll go, then."

"No, it's not that," I said. "I'd just rather not go there. I don't want to have indigestion all afternoon."

He grinned. "Know what you mean," he said, tossing a lock of his gorgeous golden hair over his forehead in a way that made me go quivery inside. "Where *would* you like to go, then?"

It was a nice day for November – cold and breezy, but sunny. "Why don't we grab some sandwiches from the shop and we'll take them into the park? We could sit by the pond—"

"And throw crusts for the ducks. OK," he agreed.

I felt proud to be holding Sim's hand as we walked across the muddy grass, taking a short cut to the pond. We were still quite a way off when I spotted an empty bench. Three girls from my school were also heading towards it.

"Quick!" I said, breaking into a run and tugging him along.

We got there just ahead of the others and claimed the bench, panting and laughing. The girls glared at us. They were from the year below mine.

"First come, first served," I said airily, and they walked off, muttering.

We cracked open our cans of soft drink and nibbled our sandwiches. When we'd finished eating, he slid his arm along the back of the bench, then dropped it on to my shoulders and squeezed them.

"Well, when am I going to see you again?" he asked me.

"You're seeing me now, aren't you?" I answered, but my heart was thumping like mad as he said the words I'd hoped he'd say.

"I mean, properly. Like, in the evening, on a date, just us two, not a whole parkful of people."

I rested my head against his shoulder. "Tonight?" I suggested hopefully.

"Great. Let's go to Smilers."

I frowned worriedly. "I'm a bit broke," I said. Smilers was a really great club, but the drinks were expensive.

"Don't worry about that," Sim said.

"How will I get in? You're supposed to be over eighteen. What if they ask for ID?" I said.

"Don't worry, I'll take care of it. I know a bloke on the door," he said.

I was still doubtful. I was only just seventeen and I thought I looked young for my age.

"Don't look so worried! We'll have a great time," Sim assured me.

And we did. His mate on the door let us in with no problems. The music was fantastic and we kissed so much that my lips felt sore. At the end of the evening, I was on a real high. I had a wonderful, great-looking boyfriend, so the Gang of Three couldn't torment me any more. For years they'd picked on me, telling me I'd never find a boyfriend and that ugly, skinny girls like me should become nuns. Now I could get one over on them by sauntering past hand in hand with Sim and proving I wasn't a failure with boys after all!

For the next couple of months, things were fantastic. Sim bought me a fabulous Christmas present – three CDs which I really wanted, and a velvet scarf. I felt he really cared about me.

I couldn't see him every night as I had loads of homework to do, and so did he, with his

A levels in just four months' time. Seeing Sim and fitting in my homework left little time for seeing friends. Normally, I'd have gone out with Lori on Friday evenings, which was when Carl saw his mates, but Friday was now a Sim night. Lori had grumbled a lot at first, but now she seemed to accept the fact that, as well as being her friend, I was part of a couple and had other obligations.

At the end of each date, and every walk, we would cling to each other and kiss, but if his hands strayed anywhere, I always pushed them away. I didn't want to get groped in the park, or on the doorstep.

When he asked me why I wouldn't let him touch me, I always gave the same reply: that I was scared someone might see. He seemed to accept that I was shy, and that was fine by me.

I was dying to meet his parents and sisters and see what kind of house he lived in. I wondered when he was going to invite me home to meet them.

Then, one Sunday, it happened. I was at home, down on my stomach on the carpet, wriggling around, pretending to be a dragon while the twins rode on my back, when Ollie, my eldest brother, yelled that there was a phone call for me.

"Who is it?" I screeched. "If it's Lori, tell her I'll

ring her back."

"It's some bloke," Ollie shouted.

I leapt up, dislodging Jamie, who started to wail, and losing a chunk of my hair which Jo-Jo refused to let go of. With a smarting scalp, I raced to the phone.

"Ollie, go and keep an eye on those two, will you?" I said. He started to protest that he was in the middle of something else.

"Just *do* it, will you?" I snapped. I was sick and tired of being the only one except Mum who seemed to do anything useful around the place.

"Sorry about that," I said down the receiver.

Sim's voice replied, "Have I caught you at a bad moment?"

I sighed deeply. "Every moment's a bad moment in our house."

"Then here's your knight on a white charger, offering you an escape route. How would you like to come to my place for lunch today?"

Getting to Sim's wasn't easy. It involved a bus journey and a long walk. I got there at around a quarter past one, hoping against hope that I hadn't held up his family's Sunday meal.

Sim opened the door to me himself. I could hear Oasis blaring in the background. The house was on one of those new estates where all the houses look exactly the same, and all the front gardens are open plan and scattered with straggly rose bushes and half-dead saplings with piles of dog poo round their roots.

There were pictures of dogs in Sim's front hall, but he said they didn't have one any more – they'd had to get rid of it before they moved here.

He led me into a long, narrow lounge that ran the full length of the house and had windows either end. It had a horrid, knobbly, tufty carpet, in a nasty slug colour, sort of greyish brown, and the three-piece suite was tan and also covered in tufts and fringes. I didn't blame Sim. I knew he hadn't chosen the furnishings.

"Where is everyone?" I asked, surprised that none of his family had come to greet me.

"They've all gone out for the day," he replied. "I didn't want to go. I thought it would give us a chance to be alone together."

"What for?" They were the most stupid words that had ever left my lips.

Sim walked towards me with a smile on his face. He held out his arms. "You know what for," he said.

I went ice-cold with shock. Then, as panic hit me, I started to shake.

"What's wrong?" Sim asked concernedly.

"You've gone pale."

He tried to pull me to him but I was as stiff as a plank of wood. He planted a kiss on my lips but I was completely unresponsive.

"Why are you trembling?" he asked me.

I shook my head and stared down at my feet. He must have thought me a real wimp. I wouldn't have minded betting that Clare, a friend of Lori's who was mad on him, would have given anything for a chance like this. She'd probably have been lying starkers on the sofa by now, saying, "Take me, I'm yours!"

Sim had another go at trying to kiss me. This time, I actually managed to get my mouth to move a little. He started stroking my back, as if I were a nervous cat.

"Come on, that's better," he said.

I let him kiss me, but when he started steering me over to the sofa, I froze again.

He let go of me and stared at me. "Look, Rachel, what's wrong? I know something is. . ." he said.

How could I tell him? How could I admit I was terrified of being all alone in the house with my boyfriend?

"Would you like me to draw the curtains? Is that it? Maybe you'd rather go up to my bedroom."

"No!" I practically screamed at him.

He took a step back, shocked at my violent reaction to his suggestion.

"M-maybe I'd better go home," I mumbled, picking my bag up from the chair where I'd dumped it when I came in.

"Is this your way of telling me we're finished?" Sim's grey eyes were smoky-dark like storm clouds and his lips were set and angry.

I shook my head and stood uncertainly in the doorway. I honestly didn't know what to do. I was on the verge of tears. Then they welled up and I couldn't hold them back. My bag fell to the floor as I covered my face with my hands and sobbed.

I felt Sim's arms go round me and hold me tight. Then he stroked my hair. I leaned against him, all the strength and fight gone out of me. This time, when he steered me over to the sofa, I let my knees sag and slumped on to it.

Sim sat down beside me, still holding me. Suddenly, he stood up, went into the kitchen and returned with a roll of kitchen towel, white with little red rosebuds on it. He tore off a piece. I took it and blew loudly. The red rosebuds made it look as if my nose was bleeding.

"Thanks," I said, sniffing.

"Rachel, what is all this about?" he asked me. "Have I done something wrong? Have I said something?"

"It's nothing to do with you. It's me," I said. I shrugged helplessly and gazed at him, my eyes wide and pleading. If only he could read my mind and spare me the embarrassment of spelling it out, I thought longingly. But he just stared at me blankly, waiting.

In the end, I took a deep breath. "It's . . . it's. . ." I began.

It was no good, the words just wouldn't come out. I licked my lips and swallowed hard. I had to tell him. I owed it to him.

My voice came out hoarse and husky. "I . . . I'm scared. I've never been alone in a house with a boy before. I haven't told you this before because I was afraid you'd laugh, but – you see, you're my first boyfriend."

He was still looking at me as if he didn't understand. I had to take the final step – the final risk. Maybe he'd laugh. Maybe he'd finish with me on the spot.

"I'm – well, I'm still a virgin."

Chapter 3

Sim sat unmoving as if he'd been paralysed. His face was set in a kind of non-expression, his mouth part open, his eyes just staring. My heart was thudding so fast with nerves that I felt faint.

Then he blinked and came back to life. He closed his mouth and licked his lips.

"Well," he said. "Well. . ."

I chewed my bottom lip, hardly realizing I was doing it until it began to feel sore, so I stopped.

"Well what?" I whispered. I had to know, I *had* to.

"I'm just a bit surprised," he said. "I thought. . ." He stopped.

I frowned. "What did you think?" I asked him.

He shrugged and gave no explanation.

"Why should you be surprised?" I persisted.

"A lot of girls my age are still virgins."

Sim leaned towards me and gave my limp hand a quick squeeze. "I didn't mean that," he said. "What I mean is, I'm surprised you told me. I'm pleased. It means you must trust me, if you can confide something like that in me. I feel privileged."

"I just wanted you to understand," I told him.

"And I do. I'm not going to rush you into anything before you're ready, Rachel. I'm not that sort of guy. There's more to relationships than sex. If all I wanted was sex, I'd finish with you now, wouldn't I?"

"Why?" I asked, startled. Then, an instant later, I thought, *What a thick question!* But it was too late. I'd said it.

Sim laughed. "Because I'd know I wasn't going to get it," he said.

I hated hearing something as important and momentous as sex referred to as "it". It diminished it, made it seem nothing, something to throw away like a piece of crumpled paper. But I didn't confide these thoughts to Sim. Instead, I just let out a deep sigh.

Sim stood up. "Can I get you a drink? Tea? Coffee? Coke?"

"All in one cup?" I joked. It was something my grandad used to say. He died last year. I felt a quick pang as his face swam into my mind's eye. He hadn't been that old, either: sixty-eight, four times older than I was now. I remembered how Mum had cried.

I decided on coffee and Sim went to make it. While he was in the kitchen, I got up and roamed around the room, looking for clues about his life. There were some framed photographs on the mantelpiece. One was of a couple on their wedding day, obviously Sim's parents. His mother had short, curly blonde hair and his father was equally fair. There was another one of three little blond children, Sim and his sisters, looking cute as they nibbled candyfloss at a fair.

Sim came back with the coffees. I sat back on the sofa but Sim parked himself on a chair by the window. He had a packet of chocolate biscuits and he offered me one.

"No thanks," I said. I couldn't have eaten. I'd have choked on the crumbs.

He ate three, then folded the wrapper over at the end and gave it a twist. It was something I did, too, and it made him feel familiar, so that I felt closer to him. I began to relax again.

He leaned back in his chair and crossed his legs lazily. "I really like you, Rachel, I want you to know that," he said.

I murmured, "Thanks," and felt my face heat

up. He'd said "like", but he hadn't said, "love". Or was he leading up to that? To hide my confusion, I blew on the surface of my hot coffee, creating mini waves in my mug. Some went over the edge and splashed on to my skirt.

"Damn!" I exclaimed.

Sim smiled. "Shall I get a cloth?" he offered.

I shook my head. "I'll stick it in the washing-machine when I get home," I told him.

He put his mug on the window-sill, stood up and came over to where I was sitting. "Shove over," he said.

I slithered to one end of the sofa and he sat so close that our sides were touching. His arm slid around my back and he pulled me close and turned me so that I was facing him. I just had time to put my mug down on the coffee table before he kissed me.

It was a long, long kiss from which I thought I'd never surface. I didn't want to. But both of us had to breathe.

"That's better," Sim said softly.

"Yes," I whispered, snuggling against him.

"I really want to make love to you," he said. "Please don't make me wait too long."

He stroked my hair and I shivered. Then, speaking close to my ear, he murmured, "I know you'll be worth waiting for, Rachel."

30

He blew on the back of my neck, making me shiver again.

Shortly after that, I told him I'd better be getting home and he walked me to the bus-stop, saying he was going to call round to see a mate of his.

When I got back, the house was empty. The Slob Bros were out and so were Mum and the twins. I decided to ring Lori and tell her the latest developments. She must have been through this state, too, before she started sleeping with Carl.

I counted the rings, held my breath as the phone was picked up at the other end, and let it out again in relief when I found it was Lori. "Hello, stranger," she said. "Long time no phone."

It was true, I thought guiltily. I had been neglecting her and was only ringing because I wanted something. But this wasn't the time for a discussion about our friendship.

"Can you talk without anyone overhearing?" I asked her.

"Sure. I'll take the phone into my bedroom," she assured me.

"Lori, can you remember when you first made love with Carl?" I asked her.

She giggled.

"I'm serious," I said.

"What do you need to know for?"

I told her about Sim wanting us to have sex.

"How long did you know Carl for, before it happened?" I asked her.

"Four months," she replied promptly. My eyebrows shot up. It didn't seem very long. I'd only known Sim for a couple of months. Was there some kind of code about sex, so that boys were prepared to wait a certain amount of time, but no longer?

"Well, I want to wait another three months, at least! Do you think Sim will get fed up?" I said.

"Look, it's not all down to what Sim wants. What do *you* want?" Lori asked me.

"I'd rather wait a bit," I replied. "I don't want him to get the wrong idea."

I heard Lori give a sigh. "What do you mean, the wrong idea? You're going out together, aren't you? There aren't any rules about it, it just happens. Carl and I just felt like doing it one evening, so we did. I suppose the time must have been right, or something."

"Mmm," I agreed absently. I was wondering if they'd done it on the sofa, or in bed, or what. Then I thought about Sim and me on his sofa.

"Rachel? You've gone awfully quiet. Are you still there?" Lori's voice squawked down the receiver.

"Er . . . yes," I said, dragging myself out of my fantasy.

"What's stopping you? What are you scared of?" Lori asked.

"I . . . er . . . well, that Sim might think I was easy," I ventured. It was something I worried about.

Lori gave a loud guffaw. "You've been going out for a few months now. Everyone probably thinks you're doing it already!" I hoped she was only joking.

"Then there's getting pregnant," I said.

"Condoms," was her short, sharp reply.

"I do read magazines, you know," I said, a bit huffily.

"Yes, but boys don't. It's up to you to make sure they use them," she pointed out.

"All I really want to know is, how do you know when it's the right time to do it?" I said. "That's one thing magazines never talk about."

"No one can tell you that. You just know," she said mysteriously. Then she changed the subject and began trying to pin me down to a night we could go out on the town together. I didn't want to. What was the point, now that I had Sim?

After I'd rung off, I wondered why I'd bothered to ask Lori. She was only my age, after all. How could she possibly be an expert in sex?

What I needed was a proper agony aunt.

Of course! I raced to my room and began flicking through my heap of magazines. Then I found a pen and searched for a notepad.

Dear Tricia, I began. *I'm thinking of making love with my boyfriend.*

There I stopped, pen poised. Did I mean that? I wondered. Was I really thinking of it? The pen sagged from my fingers. I put it down on the bed and stared at the words I'd written. They seemed so cold and clinical. Surely you didn't "think of making love". If you were in love with someone, it just happened, like Lori said.

I tore the page from the pad, crushed it into a ball and threw it into my waste-paper bin. I'd got the question wrong, I realized now. It should have been, *How do I know if I'm in love?* Because Lori was wrong; there *were* rules to the love game. They were ones which every individual made for him- or herself. And mine had always been, "I don't want to *make* love till I'm *in* love."

And was I? In love, that was? I honestly didn't know. My heart skipped about inside my chest when I saw Sim. It was a thrill being with him. Was that love? I had nothing to compare it to, so how did I know?

Until I *did* know for sure, if Sim asked me

again to make love with him, my answer just had to be, "No." It was the only way I could stay true to myself. When you were confused and didn't know what to do, at least being true to your own feelings was something you could grab on to and keep.

But next day, I felt even that small measure of control slipping from my grasp, because I found Sim waiting for me as I rolled up to school, and he had something in his hand: a small, gift-wrapped package.

Chapter 4

My feet slowed to a halt as I gazed at the object he was holding out to me.

"Go on, take it," he said.

"What is it?" I asked hesitantly.

"Something for you. I bought it specially."

A horrible, suspicious thought struck me. Surely he hadn't gift-wrapped a packet of condoms, in the hope of persuading me to go to bed with him?

I took the tiny package. The gold gift-wrap glinted in the strong sunlight.

"I must dash. I'll see you at lunchtime," he said, and tore off up the steps, taking them three at a time and leaving me standing, staring bemusedly at his gift.

"What's that, Rachel?" Shaz, one of Rosie's

Gang of Three, had come up behind me and I hadn't heard her. "Sim's given Rachel an engagement ring!" she yelled to Barbie, the third member of the gang.

I liked Barbie. She was quiet, softly spoken and much nicer than Rosie or Shaz, who she hung round with. I couldn't think what she saw in them, unless they'd bullied her into being friends with them.

"It's not an engagement ring," I said hotly.

"How do you know? You haven't even opened it yet!" Shaz pointed out. "Well, go on, let's see," she insisted.

Barbie tugged at her friend's arm. "Leave Rachel alone," she said.

Shaz gave her a withering look. I put the package in my pocket and glared at her. Then one of the teachers walked up and asked us to hurry along. Saved!

I didn't get a chance to open it till morning break, when I locked myself in one of the toilets and unpicked the Sellotape. It peeled off the shiny surface easily. I parted the paper and saw that I was holding a tiny, pale blue cardboard box with the name and address of a high street jeweller's printed on it in silver lettering.

I began to shake. Maybe Shaz was right!

What would I do if Sim asked me to get engaged to him?

Someone banged loudly on the cubicle door and yelled, "Hurry up!"

"Go away!" I yelled back. "Some things can't be hurried!"

With trembling fingers, I opened the box, crushing the fragile lid in the process, and, with a mixture of disappointment and relief, saw that it wasn't a sparkling ring that nestled on the blue velvet inside, but a gold chain with a tiny locket.

I stared at it with my nose wrinkled. Lockets were dead old fashioned. No one wore them any more. Didn't Sim know that?

But it was very romantic of him, all the same. I expected he wanted me to wear it in secret, with a picture of him inside. I opened it, to see if he'd already put one in, but he hadn't. The thin gold casing – was it real gold or just fake? – winked hollowly back at me.

I stuffed the empty box and the wrapping paper into the waste bin and put the locket in the pocket of my bottle green school skirt. During the next class, I kept feeling it, cold and hard against my fingertips.

Sim was waiting at the end of the corridor when classes finished for the morning. He was looking ultra cool, leaning one shoulder against the wall, his hands in his pockets. I raised my hand to wave to him, but just as I did so, I saw Rosie Francks bustle up to him and say something. I bristled. That girl meant trouble. She was bound to be stirring it in some way.

I saw her go off, and saw him laughing. He was still grinning to himself when I reached him.

"What was all that about?" I enquired airily.

"Since when have we been engaged?" he said.

"Since never!" I snorted.

"So why was Rosie congratulating me? I hope you haven't got any ideas of becoming a teenage bride!"

He laughed again and I couldn't help laughing too as I explained that Shaz had seen him give me the present and had jumped to an utterly stupid conclusion.

"Did you like your present?" he asked me.

"It's lovely," I replied.

"I'm glad. I'm no good at writing love letters, so I thought I'd give you a love token instead."

I stared at him, my pulse racing. Love . . . he'd mentioned the word love! Did this mean. . .?

"Come on," he said, grabbing my hand. "Let's go get some fresh air. It stinks of sweating brains in here."

We bought sandwiches and went into the

park. We walked much farther than usual, up the hill and down a path where people were exercising their dogs and there wasn't a soul from school to be seen.

Sim stopped and pulled me under a weeping willow tree. We stood close to the trunk, hidden inside the drooping fronds. He brushed his lips softly against mine. Then he said, "Give me the locket."

I obediently took it out of my pocket and handed it to him.

He undid the clasp and placed the chain round my neck. He had some trouble fastening it – "These thin chains are too fiddly for hunky male fingers," he joked – but in the end he managed it and I felt the locket fall against the thin skin of my breastbone. It felt cold and strange at first, then, as it warmed up, it felt as if I had always worn it.

"Could I have a photo of you to put inside?" I asked him.

"I'll see if I can find you one small enough," he said.

"If you can't, I'll bring my camera to school and get you to stand a long way away," I told him.

"That's not where I want to be," he said, and there was something husky and intimate in his tone that made the surface of my skin rise and bristle. My breath caught in my throat and I stared at him, waiting for him to continue, trying to anticipate what he might say.

"I'd much rather be close to you," he murmured. "As close as I can get."

He pulled me tightly against him and I wrapped my arms round his waist. His eyes were closed, his breathing harsh and fast. His mouth pressed against mine and he sucked my lower lip in between his lips and moved it around inside his mouth in such a sexy way that I could hardly bear it. I was getting feelings I'd never had before. Strange tingles and trembles.

I couldn't bear it and I pushed him away. "Stop it! There are people looking," I said.

"See you tonight, then?" he asked me.

I nodded and said, "All right." I had an essay that just had to be written, but that didn't mean we couldn't spend *part* of the evening together.

I was first out of school and I hung around at the bottom of the steps, watching everyone else leave. Rosie Francks and Shaz noticed me. Rosie, maybe hoping to embarrass me in front of other people, shouted, "Waiting for your fiancé, Rachel? Can I be a bridesmaid?"

I gave her a withering look. People like her were just pathetic. I felt much more confident since getting Sim's present and knowing he loved me. The Gang of Three couldn't upset me now. I'd got my very own boyfriend, one of the best looking guys in school, and we were going steady. I was every bit as good as them!

At last I saw Sim coming out of the door. He ran down the steps and grabbed hold of my hand. In front of everyone, Rosie included, he kissed me on the lips.

"I've missed you all afternoon, Rachel," he said.

"I've missed you, too," I told him.

We walked to the bus-stop together. It was raining, so I put my red umbrella up and the two of us squashed under it, laughing as either one or the other of us got raindrops down our neck.

"Do you have to go straight home?" he asked me.

"It depends," I said. "You see, I've got this bloody essay to do."

"Let's work for two hours, then ring each other," he suggested and I agreed, though I had a horrible feeling that my essay would take all night.

The theme of my essay was how the Second World War had changed the eating habits of Britain. I had a sudden brainwave and phoned my gran. Then, armed with information about dried egg powder and the fact that bananas didn't hit the greengrocers' shelves until 1954, I bashed the computer keyboard and ran my hasty words through the spell-check.

Then I looked at my watch. Ten past eight. I was starving as I'd skipped tea, and Sim hadn't rung.

When I rang him, his mother answered. "I'm afraid he went out about half an hour ago," she spoke into my incredulous ears.

"What?" I almost squeaked. "What about the translation he had to do?"

"He finished it. Then he said he was going for a walk with Amanda."

Amanda? Sim had a sister called Mandy. Maybe their parents called her Amanda. Sim's proper name was Simon and, come to think of it, I'd heard his mum call him that. My own mum had always called Oliver Ollie, and Carol-Ann was often referred to as C.A. for short. I was glad I didn't get called Rache. I'd have hated that.

"They didn't say where they were going," Sim's mum added, most helpfully. Not.

"I see. Well, thanks," I said dully, then went back to my bedroom in a gloom.

I could hear the thump-thump of one of Pete's

records coming from his room up in the attic. Our house is very old, with lots of small, dark rooms. Ollie had taken over the back downstairs living-room as his den. My bedroom is at the back, which is great because you can't hear the traffic, only the birds and people's lawn-mowers. But it's possible to feel seriously alone in the world when you're sitting at the open window, staring at the trees and wondering why your boyfriend hasn't rung you when he said he would, and has gone out without telling you. I felt really wounded. After such a sexy, loving day, too!

I fingered the locket he'd given me, polishing it between my thumb and my fingers as if it were magic and I could expect a genie to materialize. But I didn't want a genie offering me three wishes, I just wanted Sim. Why had he let me down? Why go out with his sister when he could have been seeing me? No doubt there would be some logical explanation and I'd forgive him, but right now my heart was aching and all I wanted to do was cry.

Chapter 5

I deliberately made myself late for school by waiting in to see if Sim would ring me. But he didn't. My form teacher, Mrs Doyle, was already most of the way down the register by the time I got into the classroom.

"Sorry," I apologized.

I noticed Lori scribbling something. She stuffed a piece of paper into my hand as we were walking to morning Assembly. She wasn't looking very pleased with life, I observed. In fact, she was positively glowering.

I read the note as the Head was going on about the behaviour of a group of Year Five boys who had been smoking on a bus and had sworn at the driver when he told them it wasn't allowed. It said:

Dear Rachel,

I thought we were meant to be best friends, but ever since you started going out with Sim, I hardly ever see you or hear from you, unless you want something. I never thought you were the type who dropped your friends as soon as you met a boy. I still see my friends, although I'm going out with Carl. If you really value our friendship, tell Sim you can't see him this dinnertime and spend some time with me.

Lori.

She was right, I thought guiltily. I had to let Sim know I couldn't see him, so I wrote him a note which said:

Dear Sim,

Can't see you this dinnertime, I'm afraid, as Lori wants to talk to me about something important. See you after school tonight, I hope.

Lots of love, Rachel XXXXX

I looked out for him as I changed rooms between classes and managed to catch him as he was going into the gym, looking a real babe in his navy shorts and red T-shirt. I thrust the note into his hand, smiled and dashed off again. I didn't have a chance to speak to him as Mr Tate, our English teacher, is really strict about us being

46

punctual for lessons and the last thing I wanted was to be given an extra essay to write!

"So!" Lori said accusingly as we settled ourselves on to one of Casa Gut-rot's hard wooden benches. "I suppose it's breaking your heart, spending a whole lunch hour without Sim. It really must be love."

Her tone was so sarcastic that I almost got up and left. Then I remembered she had a justified grievance and it was up to me to smooth things over and save our friendship.

"It is, Lori. I'm crazy about him. I can't think of anybody else."

"Well, that's obvious," she said, still in that sarky voice.

I steeled myself to carry on. "Look, I'm sorry if you think I've been neglecting you. I just don't seem to have time for anything—"

"Except seeing precious Sim! I wouldn't rely on him being there for you always, you know."

I stared at her. "What do you mean?"

"Oh, nothing. You know what boys are like: they can never be trusted," she replied airily. "What I really want to know is, have you two done it yet?"

I didn't like the way she put it. It made it seem crude and meaningless. My disapproval must have shown in my face, because she added, "Oh. Have I said something I shouldn't?"

I replied, "No, you haven't. And *we* haven't."

She looked disappointed. Maybe she was looking forward to having someone to share secrets about sex with, and I'd let her down. Well, she would just have to wait.

"You've had your hair cut. It looks nice," I said, in an attempt to mollify her and lighten the atmosphere. "I spy a highlight." Her light brown hair had definite blonde streaks in it.

"I thought you hadn't noticed," she said, pleased that I had.

So the subject was changed and we were back on safe ground, talking about hair and holidays. Her parents had booked a villa in Majorca. Originally, Lori had mentioned that perhaps I'd like to come too, but she hadn't said any more about it, so I assumed the offer was no longer there.

My own family never went anywhere as Mum couldn't afford it. Anyway, travelling with the twins was a nightmare. I wouldn't have wanted to spend an entire week – or, even worse, a fort-night – helping Mum look after them, with no means of escape. I didn't even want to go to Majorca now, anyway, as it would mean I'd be away from Sim. So, if Lori did repeat the invitation, I would have to let her down yet again. . .

At a quarter to four I hung round the school gates, waiting for Sim to emerge. As soon as I caught a glimpse of his blond head, my heart skipped a beat. Then I remembered I was cross with him because he hadn't rung, and tried not to look too delighted as he walked up to me.

"Who went out with their sister last night and forgot to phone me?" I greeted him accusingly.

A puzzled frown creased his brow.

"I rang you. Your mum said you'd gone out with Amanda."

His face cleared. "Yes, that's right. She was down in the dumps and wanted someone to go to the pub with. I sort of got dragged off and had no time to ring you and it was too late when we got back."

"OK, I forgive you. We do have to make space for other people sometimes," I said, thinking of Lori.

I tucked my arm in his. He dropped a kiss on the top of my head. "What did Lori want?" he asked.

I shrugged. "Nothing much. Just a chat. She says I've been ignoring her lately." I didn't think I'd better tell him that she wanted all the intimate details of our sex life!

Without slowing his stride, Sim delivered a bombshell. "Maybe we shouldn't see each other so often, then. Give ourselves more time for our friends."

I stopped in my tracks, almost tripping him up, as a horrible chill spread over me. Not see each other so often? Was this the beginning of the end?

"Mine have been complaining that they hardly ever see me these days, either. Perhaps we should sacrifice Fridays. We do see each other on Saturdays, after all," he went on.

The thought was appalling. It was just about possible to live from Monday to Friday without spending a whole evening together in between. We often had to do that because of Sim's A level studies. But Monday to Saturday? That was five whole nights!

Sim must have seen the agonized look that twisted my face, because he laughed and said, "Cheer up! This won't last for ever. One day my A levels will be over and then we can have all the time in the world to spend together."

It was only January. A levels didn't begin till May. It seemed like eternity. Still, I glued on a rigid smile and did my best to obey his order to cheer up.

Over the next three weeks, things went on much as usual, except that I did manage to see Lori one Friday, when Sim was seeing his friends. And on two occasions I met Kirsty and Mary.

Mary, like Carol-Ann, had hair I'd have died for. Hers was jet black and so shiny it looked as if she'd polished it. It was heavy hair, that hung obediently around her face and never seemed to move.

Kirsty, like me, had the opposite problem. She'd used hair relaxants but still had a mop of frizz. "Why did I have to have a dad from Ghana?" she complained. "It's all his fault!"

I didn't even have that excuse. I just had bad hair.

The second time the three of us got together, we sat in Kirsty's bedroom, having girlie chats about our hair and beauty problems. And boys. Mary was in love with the boy next door, who didn't seem to have noticed she existed, despite having lived there for six years. Kirsty had just broken up with her boyfriend, Derek.

"Never trust a man," she said to me. "All those times he said he was going to football practice, he was really seeing this posh bird who lives in one of those detached houses up on Blackbird Hill. I only found out because I went to meet him at the sports field and he wasn't there and the others told me he'd never even been asked to join the team!"

"You could say he scored an own goal," I said and even Kirsty managed to laugh. I felt sorry for her, though. How could Derek have two-timed her like that? What a bastard!

I was beginning to like them more and more. They were easy-going, much more so than Lori, who seemed so intense about everything these days. Mary said she'd caught her talking to Shaz, one of the Gang of Three, on more than one occasion. I thought she needed her head examining to be having anything to do with that lot and I decided to be a bit more careful about what I said to her in future. Though it was difficult withholding information from Lori. She was a very dominating character and hard to say no to.

It was the third Saturday in February, two days after our three-month anniversary, when it happened. He'd asked me round to his place and I'd arrived with a couple of CDs I was lending him so he could tape them.

The house was empty, apart from him.

"Mum and Dad are at Gran's. She lives in Hereford so they're staying the night," he said.

"Mel's gone with them —" Melanie was his oldest sister — "and Mandy's at an all-night party. So we've got the place to ourselves."

It was exactly like that first time I'd gone round to Sim's, when I was so scared of being alone with him. Only now I wasn't. I knew him that much better — knew that he loved me as much as I loved him.

He started talking about food, whether I'd prefer a take-away or whether we should go out to eat. As he talked, I watched his face, so animated, his grey eyes sparkling, his smile curving his cheeks. Suddenly, he fell silent.

"Why are you looking at me like that?" he asked.

"Like what?" I answered, feeling a pulse beat in my tense throat.

"You look like a wild animal that's eyeing me up for dinner."

"Well, you *were* talking about food!" I joked. Had the hunger in my eyes been that obvious? Did he suspect that, rather than food, my appetite was for him? I'd felt so deprived of him lately, with so many nights apart. The previous night had been one of the increasingly frequent Fridays when we hadn't seen each other as he said he wanted to finish off all his work before the weekend. Now, I wanted to feel his arms

53

around me and his face pressed against mine. I wanted to feel his lips, his warm breath, his fingers running through my hair.

He left the room and came back with a bottle of chilled white wine. He applied the corkscrew and removed the cork with a pop and a flourish. Then he remembered he hadn't brought any glasses in. I followed him into the kitchen. As he was reaching up to a cupboard, I twined my arms around his waist and nuzzled my face into his back.

He lowered his raised arms and slowly turned round in my embrace. My face was pressed against his chest now. I could hear his beating heart, feel it as it pounded beneath his denim shirt. His lips foraged about in my hair, then found my forehead.

"Oh Rachel, I. . ." He stopped.

"What?" I whispered.

His grey eyes darkened with passion and I could feel his emotions pouring into me as he gazed unblinkingly into my brown ones.

"You know what I want. I want you," he said huskily.

"Oh Sim!" I clung to him, my legs trembly, my head swimming as his lips caught mine in a kiss so powerful and devastating that it was as if he was sucking out my soul.

"I love you, Rachel," he said.

"I love you, too," I whispered.

"Come on. . ." He took my hand and led me back to the living-room. Then he changed his mind. "Let's go upstairs," he said.

I could scarcely walk as I followed him up the thickly carpeted stairs. I'd been in his bedroom before, but only briefly, as it didn't seem right to spend long in there with his family downstairs, knowing we were up there together.

But now there was nobody to know, nobody to care. We were alone in the house. That was the last logical thought in my head as Sim bore me down on to the bed. I felt the weight of his body on top of me — an overpowering weight that somehow felt protective, too. I felt safe with him, safe with our love. I knew he wouldn't do anything to hurt me, or anything I didn't want to do.

But I wanted to do everything — nothing could have stopped me. At last, the time felt right.

His fingers were fumbling with the buttons of his shirt. My smaller, nimbler ones could undo them better than he could, so I gave him a hand. When he started to undress me, I froze and lay there like a statue, feeling totally in his power. I knew I had already surrendered.

When he lay over me again, I felt his skin against my body, warm, smooth, vibrant, alive.

Darts of fiery passion flashed and flickered all over my flesh. I could hear myself moaning as his fingers explored my back, then moved around, caressing me, awakening me.

Suddenly, he rolled over, away from me.

"Don't stop!" I begged him.

"Are you sure?" he asked me.

I bit my lip. A huge struggle took place in my head, a struggle between my morals and upbringing and the delicious, insistent demands of my body. *You're seventeen, you're not a child any more, you're a woman now*, I reminded myself. A woman who knows what she wants. A woman in love.

"I'm sure," I whispered.

A tender smile lit his face. He brushed the curly straggles from my hot cheeks and forehead. "Quite sure?" he asked again.

"Yes."

After that, there was no doubt about what was going to happen, and it did — wonderfully, beautifully. Afterwards, I cried. I couldn't stem the sobs. I'd crossed a threshold and it was a very moving experience.

Sim pulled on his jeans and left the room. Seeing him go, I sobbed even harder. He came back with two glasses of wine and held one to my lips.

"Th-thanks." I gave a gulp, and a watery smile, then sipped the cool liquid. It went straight to my head. All at once, I hiccuped loudly, then got the giggles.

"That's better," Sim said approvingly. "I was beginning to think I'd hurt you, or upset you. I didn't, did I?"

"No, it was just me getting all emotional," I assured him. "After all, it was my first time. . ."

"May there be many more!" he said, lifting his glass in a toast.

Chapter 6

I hadn't expected to be able to sleep at all with so much going on in my head, so I was surprised when I slept deeply that night and woke up feeling great.

After I'd washed my face that morning, I looked up and studied myself in the mirror. Did I look like a girl who had just lost her virginity? Was there any way people could tell? I didn't think I looked any different, unless the glow in my cheeks was nothing to do with the towelling I'd just given them.

I waited for Sim to ring me. I felt sure he would, after such a special evening. When it got to twenty-past two and I still hadn't heard from him, I rang him, only to be informed by his sister Mandy that he wasn't in. When I asked where he'd gone, she said that she hadn't a clue because she'd only just come in herself and her parents weren't back from Hereford yet.

Boys! I thought crossly. They were impossible. They never did what you expected them to do. Of course, there was always a chance that he was on his way over to see me. . .

But he wasn't. The afternoon passed slowly. In fact, it almost went backwards. If I hadn't known how much he loved me, I'd have assumed he didn't care. Maybe things like losing your virginity didn't matter to boys the way they mattered to girls. Perhaps last night had only been special to me.

Especially if he's slept with girls before. . .

The awful thought hammered into my head with the power of a road drill. Had he? I'd never asked. I'd assumed he was as innocent as I was. But what if he wasn't? What if he'd had loads of girls before me? What if he'd told them all he loved them?

A lump started to form in my throat and I felt my eyes grow moist. *Stop being such an idiot!* I told myself sharply. *Of course Sim loves you! He's been going steady with you since November, hasn't he?*

But where was he this afternoon? We normally did something together on Sundays, even if it was only going for a walk. Had he been so over-whelmed by last night that he needed time to think? Maybe, like me, his head was in a total whirl.

For a boy not to ring a girl the day after she'd lost her virginity to him wasn't just bad manners, it was downright heartless, I decided. Surely Sim. . . But I could carry on with "surely Sims" till the cows came home and I wouldn't be any closer to the truth. I wouldn't know till I got a chance to ask him in person.

I worried myself into a bad headache and went to bed at around nine o'clock. Then Ollie came in and started playing thumping rock music, so I had to go down and plead with him to be a bit quieter. Then one of his mates came round and the CD player was turned up again.

Pete was watching telly with Mum. "I'll sort him out," he offered.

I don't know what he said to him, but it worked and next thing I knew it was Monday morning. School. And Sim. . .

Except I was wrong about the latter: Sim wasn't at school that day.

I waited for him by the gates in the morning, almost making myself late again. I looked for him at lunchtime and finally was spotted by Lori, who insisted we eat our sandwiches together.

She thought it was funny that he was off school. "You must have worn him out!" she laughed.

By then, of course, she'd dragged a full confession out of me in her usual demanding way.

I couldn't wait for school to finish. I had decided to go to Sim's to see if he was all right. I even bought him a get-well card in case he was laid up with the flu. If he was, it would explain why he hadn't rung on Sunday.

As I was walking up his road, a car passed me. I don't know what made me look. Maybe it was the slow, slightly erratic way in which it was being driven. There was a girl at the wheel – a girl in a blue jacket, with long blonde curls cascading over her shoulders. The reason why she was driving so badly was that the man sitting beside her had his arm round her and was trying to hug her. His hair was as fair as hers. I didn't get a look at his face but a nasty shudder passed through me because he looked a bit like Sim.

The car disappeared and I carried on up the winding road through the housing estate. When I reached Sim's house, the car was nowhere to be seen.

Sim's sister Mandy answered the door. "He's

not home from school yet, Rachel," she told me.

"But – but he wasn't at school today!" I said perplexedly. "I thought perhaps he was ill."

"Sim, ill? He never gets anything wrong with him, lucky thing, apart from when he broke his ankle falling off a swing when he was five," she informed me. "Of course he was at school today. He left early this morning – said something about having to get some information from the library before a lesson. You must have missed him somehow. Would you like to come in and wait for him?"

Of course I wanted to, more than anything, but some instinct told me not to. So I shook my head and told her just to tell him I'd called.

At the bus-stop, I took the get-well card from my bag, tore it into tiny pieces and dropped them in the bin. I felt like crying. Something definitely didn't feel right. Even if Saturday hadn't happened, he would have rung or seen me by now.

I got home and couldn't eat any of the stew Mum had made for us all. I couldn't even concentrate on my homework. I'd never felt so puzzled and confused in my life. Snatches of Saturday kept coming back to me: Sim's tender words, his passionate lovemaking. It seemed so long ago now.

In the end, I decided to ring to see if he was back yet.

This time it was Sim's mother who answered. Maybe sorrow or suspicion had altered my voice in some way, because she said, "Oh, hello, Amanda. Is Sim with you? If he is, please send him home immediately. I want a word with him. If I find out he spent the day with you instead of going to school, I'm going to be very angry indeed!"

Chapter 7

I honestly thought I'd gone mad. I'd only just spoken to Amanda, his sister, alias Mandy. Surely their mother knew she was at home? And what would Amanda be doing ringing from somewhere else?

Then I remembered the car, and the blonde with the Sim look-alike. Amanda was a pretty common name. What if there were two of them – his sister, and another Amanda whom Sim was seeing? That meant he was two-timing me!

Sim's mum was still going, "Hello? Hello? Are you there?" on the other end of the phone. I was feeling so dazed, I was tempted to put it down without saying anything. But some devil in me wanted Sim to know I'd found him out.

"You've got the wrong person, Mrs Burton.

This isn't Amanda, it's Rachel," I said croakily.

There was a muffled exclamation, an "Oh, sorry!" followed by the sound of the receiver going down with a bang.

The words I thought of to describe Sim were unrepeatable. He was the lowest of the low, a complete slimy reptile. How could he two-time me after we'd just made love for the first time? Or was that all he'd ever been after? He'd worn me down, waited for me to give in to him, then dropped me. Maybe he'd been going out with this Amanda for ages and had two-timed *her* with me!

How could he have lied and said he loved me, though? He'd made a complete fool of me.

I started to cry, great, racking sobs, thinking of how taken in I'd been, how easily I'd believed his lies – believed he loved me – and how I'd given up my virginity to him so easily. Well, he was going to find out what he'd lost!

Soon, though, my tears dried as I started to get angry again. I wanted revenge. All kinds of mad ideas whizzed through my head, but I dismissed them. There was a far easier way than spiking his cola with castor oil, or spreading nasty rumours about him.

Sim wasn't the only good-looking boy in our school – or even in my street! Once he saw me going out with someone else and looking happy, instead of moping round after him and begging him to come back to me, he'd soon want me back. But he wasn't going to get me. He could beg, plead, buy me a dozen lockets and two dozen bunches of flowers, but he'd never get me to go out with him again. What we'd had for the last three months was tarnished beyond repair.

I was dreading going into school on Tuesday, knowing that Sim would definitely be there. There was no way he would play truant two days running. Sure enough, as I walked through the gates I could see him just ahead of me.

My instant reaction was to break out in a cold sweat, but I forced my shaky legs to march up to him.

"Hello, Sim." I tried to make my voice sound strong and determined, though I felt weak as a newborn lamb.

"Oh! Hi, Rachel." At least he had the grace to blush.

"So, what have *you* got to say for yourself?" I demanded angrily. Fury was filling me now. So was righteous indignation at being treated this way by him.

"I don't know what you mean," he mumbled. "Look, I'm going to be late—"

I grabbed his sleeve. "You're not going any-where till I get a few answers," I spat at him. "Who was the blonde bit I saw you in a car with on Monday? Could her name have been Amanda, by any chance?"

"She – she's just a neighbour," he stammered. "She shares a house with some other air stewardesses. She's been away for a while so when she got back, she called in and we went for a drink. That's all."

"Oh, so she's an air stewardess, is she? That explains everything!" I cried. I was aware that other people were witnessing our heated dis-cussion. It hadn't quite turned into a row yet, but it was well on the way.

"What do you mean?" he asked me.

"They've got dreadful reputations for sleeping with everyone going – passengers, other crew. I've just read an article about them in a maga-zine. It described what they get up to in foreign hotels," I told him.

Sim shrugged. "Journalists will make a sens-ation of anything," he said.

"But you were seeing her?" I pursued.

"Occasionally. Just when she was in town."

"And when was the last time?" I enquired frostily.

"About six weeks after I started going out with

you. You were still saying no to me at that point, so what's a randy lad to do? Amanda knows what it's all about. She's twenty-three. She doesn't pretend to be a prissy little virgin," he said.

"What? How dare you!" I shrieked and, with all my might, I slapped him across the face. Then I tore off the locket he'd given me, which I was still wearing. "Take this back, I don't want it," I yelled. "It's not even gold, you cheapskate!"

I'd shown it to Pete, who'd confirmed my suspicions. "You probably paid two quid for it in the market. There!" I flung it at his feet, then stamped on it.

Then, suddenly, I was overwhelmed with tears at the unfairness of what he'd said. "I – I d-didn't pretend to be a v-virgin, I was one, really and truly," I faltered, my voice choked with sobs. "Didn't – didn't you feel anything for me at all?"

I was showing my weakness by asking him that, but I couldn't help it, I just had to know.

"I liked you a lot, but I could see you were starting to fall for me. I don't want a girl in my life who's going to fall in love with me and get all soppy and possessive. It's not part of my game-plan. I'm going off to university in October. For now, I just want to have fun," he said.

"Fun. With girls like Amanda," I said dully.

"Yes, exactly. I thought you were going to be like that. Rosie and Shaz said you flirted with all the guys and that they thought you were well up for it. You certainly made me wait!"

My anger returned. "It's not true! Was that the only reason you asked me out?" I blazed at him. I had to know.

Shaz just happened to stroll by at that moment and gave us both an interested look. "Bitch!" I hurled at her. "Lying bitch!"

She gave me a lofty look, as if she were vastly superior to me, and walked on.

"One of the reasons," Sim admitted. "Plus the fact that you're quite pretty."

Quite pretty? Only *quite*? That made my blood boil. I couldn't take any more of this. It was making me late as well.

"I don't think we've got any more to say to each other," I said. "Goodbye, Sim. Good luck to you and Amanda. And the rest."

I walked off as coolly as I could, glad that I'd got the last word, even though I'd blown things by crying. But I couldn't resist a peep over my shoulder, and saw Sim pick up the bent locket and chain and stuff it into his pocket. Maybe he was going to straighten it out and pretend he'd bought it for Amanda. . .

* * *

Over the next three or four weeks, I was hit by a huge feeling of anti-climax. That Saturday when I'd let Sim make love to me represented the emotional pinnacle of my life. It had been like getting to the top of a high mountain – but I hadn't expected to topple off the peak and slide down into the valley of depression quite so soon.

If I'd thought ahead, I might have guessed that Sim wouldn't have wanted to get deeply involved, with college coming up in the autumn. If only I'd held my feelings back, looked on it as something casual – but life is full of "if onlys", as my gran once said.

My other overriding emotion was one of pure hatred towards the Gang of Three. Not Barbie, perhaps. She had always seemed much nicer than the other two. She was simply in their power and unable to break free. But Rosie and Shaz were my sworn enemies now, after the things they'd said about me. If anyone was responsible for my current unhappiness, it was them. I hoped they'd both get their own come-uppance some day soon.

Time passed in a daze of misery, soul-searching, vague revenge plans and swotting for my end-of-year exams. Our school was really piling on the work this year, determined to do well in the school league tables by showing lots of good exam passes and university entrances.

By the second week in March, blue skies and breezy sunshine had the effect of making me feel a bit perkier and better able to face the year ahead as a single girl. The two people who had helped me more than anyone, more even than Mum (who had at last lent me a listening ear when she found me sobbing in front of the telly one night), were Mary and Kirsty. They were proving really good friends. But Lori kept poking her nose in every time she saw me talking to them. She'd drag me off, as if I were her possession. She also tried to monopolize me on Friday nights and made a big fuss if I said I was seeing Kirsty and Mary.

"Look, Lori," I said to her one day, "I am allowed to have other friends, you know. I know you're friendly with other people apart from me."

I was referring obliquely to Shaz. At last I'd seen with my own eyes what Mary and Kirsty had reported, that the two of them seemed to be palling up.

"I've got to be. I hardly see anything of you,"

she said accusingly. "You might as well still be going out with Sim!"

I gave a shudder. I was doing my level best to blot him from my memory. Why did she have to remind me of him? I was beginning to feel that the two of us weren't destined to be best buddies, after all. Although she could be a laugh when she was out with you, too often she'd show her jealous, possessive side and I didn't like it one bit. So maybe I *had* been avoiding her a bit.

Despite my close friendships with my girl friends, I did miss having a special boy in my life. I needed to get my self-confidence back. They say that when you fall off a bike or a horse, you should get right back on again so you won't lose your nerve. I felt it was the same with boys. I needed to go out with someone before I was completely broken of the habit.

There was one boy I liked and fancied. His name was Lloyd Wilson and he was tall, dark-skinned, utterly hunky and one of our school's soccer stars. The bad news was that he was seldom without a girlfriend, but one morning I happened to be walking alongside him as we went up the school drive the Monday morning of the third week in March.

I realized that this was a fantastic opportunity

to see if I still had what it took to get off with a boy. After all, I was quite pretty – Sim had said so. I'd always thought of myself as ugly till he'd said that. He'd done me a favour, after all.

"Hello," I said, smiling flirtatiously.

Lloyd dragged himself out of whatever trance he was in, looked at me and said, "Hi. Rachel, isn't it?"

"Yeah. That's right," I replied. "Penny for them. . ."

"I think I've got a touch of exam anxiety," he told me.

"I know a cure for that," I said, batting my eyelashes at him. If Rosie Francks had seen me, she'd have thought all her criticisms about me throwing myself at boys were true. Because I *was* throwing myself at Lloyd. Deliberately. It was a game, but only partly. My status would improve no end if I went out with him, but I liked him, too.

"Oh yeah? What is it?" he asked me.

"A date with me!" I informed him, with a big grin. I could scarcely believe myself. I'd never have thought I'd have the guts to ask a boy out!

Lloyd grinned. "OK, you're on. When?"

I put my head on one side and tried to look as if I was mentally consulting my Filofax. Then I said, "Wednesday seems good."

"OK, Wednesday it is, then. Fancy a movie? Only there's two that I've been trying to get round to seeing. You can choose which one."

"That'd be great," I said.

His brow creased. "I thought you were going out with Sim?" he said.

"Haven't you heard? He's got another girl-friend now, an air stewardess called Amanda," I replied knowledgeably.

"That's OK then," Lloyd said. "Meet you after school on Wednesday."

"Yeah. See you!" I went happily off up the steps, feeling utterly triumphant. I'd never thought getting dates with boys was so easy. It had only needed me to make the first move.

The date went like a dream. For all his reputation for being a womanizer – or maybe because of it – Lloyd was the perfect gentleman. His manners were impeccable – opening doors, ushering me into my seat, buying me a drink and some popcorn. The film was a comedy and we had such a laugh.

Afterwards, Lloyd brought me home. He'd borrowed his brother's car and when he stopped it at the end of our street, by a wall where there are some garages, I knew what I was in for.

As soon as he started kissing me, I froze. The

last person to have kissed me was Sim and the sensations came sweeping back. It wasn't fair! I wanted to wipe every trace and memory of Sim's lovemaking from my brain and, more importantly, from my body, but it was proving only too easy to recall the warmth of his lips and the feel of his roaming caressing hands.

"Don't," I murmured weakly as Lloyd's hands began to explore too far.

Being the gentleman he was, he stopped right away. Then he said he'd like to see me again and my heart gave a little bump.

"I'd like that, too," I said.

On our next date, Lloyd took me out for a curry. He loved hot food. Unfortunately, not knowing much about Indian food, I chose a Madras and drank nearly a whole jug of water to soothe my burning mouth. Some boys would have laughed at me, but Lloyd didn't. He seemed quite upset that a meal he was treating me to had caused me such discomfort.

"It was my fault. I should have asked you which were the mild ones," I told him, as we drove home. "I've never been to a curry restaurant before. We've had take-aways at home but Mum ordered them and she must have known which dishes were OK."

I couldn't see Lloyd at weekends because he played football then. But one Saturday his match was cancelled due to bad weather and he asked me to go to a party with him. This was the fifth time we'd been out together, and two months since I'd split up with Sim.

Lori and Carl were at the party. We all had much too much to drink and I found myself alone in a bedroom with Lloyd.

The next bit is going to sound awful. I let Lloyd make love to me, and the next day I couldn't remember anything about it. I couldn't have said whether the experience was good, bad, or indifferent. All I know is that it happened, and I only know that because Lloyd rang me on the Sunday to see if I was all right – I had a crashing hangover – and said how great I'd been in bed. Great? What on earth had I done? I remembered being in the bedroom, I remembered kissing him, but after that, everything was a blank.

I prayed that Lloyd had used a condom. Thank God it was him! It was scary, thinking what might have happened if I'd gone to bed with a stranger while I was drunk, rather than Lloyd, who was a nice, caring person. You hear things about girls getting pregnant at parties and not knowing who the father is. After that Saturday night, I could understand how it could happen.

Having done it once, Lloyd naturally thought our relationship had progressed to the sexual stage and wanted to do it again. When it came down to it, I found I couldn't.

We were on the golf links on the outskirts of town. It was an unusually warm evening at the beginning of April. It was great to go out in just jeans and a sweatshirt, instead of a thick jacket. As we stood on top of a hill, looking down at the road, the canal and all the sparkling lights, Lloyd started kissing me, then led me into the shadow of the trees.

We kissed again, but when he began to unzip my jeans, I pushed his hands away.

"Why not?" he asked me, in an incredulous tone. "There's no one around!"

"I know that," I said. "It's just. . . Oh, I don't know. I don't want to, that's all."

"You just need some more persuading," Lloyd said gently, and proceeded to stroke my face and hair, and kiss me so tenderly that I felt I had no excuse not to make love. But as I lay there beneath him, I couldn't connect somehow. I felt like a stone and I didn't know why. He must have thought his great lover from Saturday night had turned into the dullest one imaginable. I couldn't speak to him afterwards, and we drove home in silence.

Maybe that was why things started cooling between us after that. He didn't ring me quite so often, and then he said his cousin Mally had come over from Jamaica and was staying with them. He brought her to a football match I went to. She was stunningly beautiful and, from the way she kissed him and twined herself round him after the match, there seemed to be a lot more than just cousinly affection between them, so I bowed out and told Lloyd I couldn't see him any more.

I felt nothing but a slight sadness. He was a really nice guy. But you can't go out – and definitely can't sleep – with someone you feel nothing for, can you? Well, I can't, anyway. I wondered whether I was stuck with this for the rest of my life and would never, ever get any enjoyment out of sex. It was a pretty bleak prospect. I think, in my heart, I knew it was all tied up with Sim and his cruel treatment of me. Even a pleasant few weeks of dating a nice guy like Lloyd had done nothing to heal my emotions. I wondered what would.

A couple of weeks after splitting up with Lloyd, when I was still feeling worried and depressed, I found myself sitting next to Paul O'Connor on the bus home from school. Paul was the boy Lori used to fancy before she got off with Carl.

We started to chat, just ordinary talk about school. I thought nothing of it, till he suddenly asked what I was doing later.

"Nothing," I replied.

"Fancy coming to a movie?" he said.

I should have been working to finish an overdue essay, but I found myself agreeing to meet Paul instead.

I rang Lori up as soon as I got home and told her. I knew she'd be interested. She always tried to keep track of who Paul was going out with.

"I'd watch it if I were you," she said warningly, after hoping I'd enjoy the film.

"What do you mean, 'watch it'?" I demanded angrily. What on earth was she insinuating?

"Nothing," she said annoyingly. "If you don't know, then there's no point my telling you."

And that was all I could get out of her. Then.

Paul was really randy. Unlike the polite Lloyd, he made his intentions plain on the first date, as he was kissing me and trying to grope me in the cinema. I kept pushing his hands away and he, just as determinedly, kept putting them back. I got the giggles, and finally we decided to miss the end of the film, as we were getting filthy looks from people around us.

It was raining and we took shelter in a shop doorway. Paul kept telling me I was gorgeous. He put his hands inside my shirt and started fondling my breasts and I let him. Something inside me switched off again like it had done with Lloyd and I didn't try to stop Paul when he wanted to make love to me.

All at once there was a loud whistle and some boys started yelling encouragement at Paul. It was a bunch of his mates, who had just left the cinema. That was the end of our sex session as far as I was concerned. I straightened my clothes, hoping Paul's mates had thought we were only snogging, and told Paul firmly that I had to go home.

"Can I see you again?" he asked me eagerly.

"OK," I agreed. I must admit that my sudden popularity had gone to my head a bit. It was as if I'd been lost in a desert for weeks and had suddenly found an oasis. Sim had said I was quite pretty, Lloyd had called me sexy and Paul had said I was gorgeous. Maybe I wasn't as plain as I'd thought I was.

I gazed at myself in the mirror when I got home that night. I pushed my thick hair off my face. My bone structure was really quite delicate and my eyes were larger than I'd thought. Maybe, if I went for a really good haircut, I could improve my looks even more. I'd make an appointment tomorrow, I decided.

But tomorrows have a way of turning out quite unlike the way you expected them to. . .

Chapter 8

It started as soon as I walked into school. I ran straight into the guys who had walked past Paul and me in the shop doorway.

"How much for a good time, darlin'?" one of them cackled.

I gave him a filthy look and stalked past.

In the classroom, I tried to say something to Lori and she tossed her head and ignored me, and then I saw Rosie Francks and Shaz giggling.

As our form teacher called the register, I was aware of more giggles and people staring at me and I swiftly examined what I was wearing, in case my skirt was tucked into my knickers or someone had pinned a notice on my back saying, KICK HERE.

Everything seemed in order. Yet even people

from other years were staring at me in the school hall, and as I was walking back to my classroom.

At break, I finally saw it – well, one of them. A notice taped to the wall just outside our classroom said, in straggly black felt tip, RACHEL KELLY IS A SLAG. SHE'S SLEPT WITH THE FOLLOWING BOYS. A list of boys' names followed. It included Sim, Lloyd, Paul and even mentioned the school caretaker, Mr Barlow.

I ripped it down, my face flaming. But there was another, larger one outside the gym, featuring a caricature of me wearing stockings, suspenders and a bra. An even worse one was outside the boys' toilets. CALL RACHEL FOR A GOOD TIME, it proclaimed, and then gave my phone number.

I was devastated. All I wanted to do was hide away from the human race. I raced off to the loo, locked myself into a cubicle and burst into tears.

Kirsty and Mary came after me.

"Rachel! Rachel, are you all right? Come out!" Kirsty kept calling.

"No, I'm not coming out. I'm never coming out. I can't!" I wailed tragically.

I heard them talking to each other. They didn't know what to do. Then other people came in and I could hear myself being discussed in muttering voices, though I couldn't hear what everybody said.

When I heard somebody mention fetching one of the teachers, I knew the time had come to emerge. Kirsty and Mary were still there.

"I just want to go home. I never want to set foot in here again," I sobbed.

Mary put an arm round me. She was being so kind, considering what a disgusting slag I was supposed to be. "Splash your face with cold water, it'll make you feel better," she suggested in her practical way.

I took her advice and did feel a bit better, though only physically.

"How can I carry on today, knowing everyone in the school's seen those notices?" I wailed.

"I'm sure they haven't all seen them," Mary said.

"It's not true! I'm not a slag!" I insisted, but my protest sounded half-hearted, even to my ears, because all at once I felt terribly guilty. After all, I'd slept with two boys in two months, and had gone a long way with a third. That was pretty dreadful of me.

It was so unfair, though, I thought miserably. If a boy slept with lots of girls, his mates envied his success and thought of him as some kind of hero. But if a girl did it, she was a tart. What had happened to equality of the sexes?

It took every ounce of my courage to walk out of the toilets and face the school. Even though the notices outside the gym and the boys' toilets had been taken down, there might be others elsewhere which I hadn't seen. It was obvious to me who the culprits were – those boys who had seen Paul and me half undressed in the doorway the previous night. They might have been watching us for some time, for all I knew.

As I walked down the corridors towards my classroom, I tried to keep looking straight ahead. I didn't want to make eye contact with anybody. Mary and Kirsty were still with me. We'd always been quite good friends, but suddenly I felt they were really good ones, and I'd never noticed. Where was Lori in my hour of need? She was supposed to be my best friend. I would have thought that, if anyone had stuck by me and tried to comfort me, it would have been her.

Outside the physics lab, I suddenly spotted another notice and felt sick. SLAGGY KELLY HAS GREAT TITS, it proclaimed, and below the words was a crude drawing of naked breasts. Mary ripped it down for me, crumpled it into a ball and shoved it into her bag, while Kirsty gave my shoulders a squeeze.

"They're not worth bothering about. They're scum, the people who did this," she assured me.

I knew they were, but it didn't make me feel any better.

I was still red-eyed at dinnertime and terrified of bumping into any of the boys. All I wanted to do was get right away from school, but I couldn't. I was forced to stay there for the rest of the afternoon, as I had a really important class in which our French teacher was going to go through our translations of Verlaine.

My eyes scanned the walls as I walked towards the classroom, to see if I could spot any more of the nightmare notices. There weren't any, thank goodness. Presumably, the person who'd put them up had been too busy to do any more, or else my persecution had ended.

Suddenly, I saw Lori coming out of the library.

"Thanks for looking after me this morning. Not." I gave her a hurt look.

She looked away. We walked down the corridor together, but we could have been ten miles apart.

"What's wrong? Don't you want to be seen in the company of the school slag?" I said sarcastically.

She stopped walking. We were at a kind of T-junction at the end of a corridor. One side of the T, the short side, went to two classrooms at the end, while the longer side went off past some more classrooms and finished up at the main entrance.

"Look, Rachel, if you're thinking I had anything to do with those notices, I hadn't, but you can't say you didn't deserve it," she said accusingly. "Whoever put those notices up was right. You *have* been acting like a slag!"

"Lori!" I was so beside myself with fury that I almost hit her. "How dare you!" I shouted. "You were the one who said I had to tell you everything that was going on, otherwise I wasn't a true best friend. And then you throw it back in my face like this! What the hell was I supposed to do?"

Her face was red with anger. "I always admired you, Rachel. I thought you were so cool, so sensible. Then you suddenly go mad, just because you've discovered sex."

"I haven't 'gone mad', as you put it," I protested through gritted teeth. "Maybe it's you who are mad, going out with the same boy for so long, at your age. Maybe you should be playing the field a bit."

"What? And end up a slag like you? No thanks!"

Lori really had declared war now. Our friendship was at an end and I told her so.

All the while we were arguing, people kept walking past and staring at us.

Lori turned and started to walk away. Then she turned back to face me. "Rosie and Shaz agree with me. They think you're a slag, too," she said, in her most insulting tones.

"*You told Rosie Francks?*" I screamed hysterically. I was totally beside myself with fury. I'd told her in strictest confidence. How could she have repeated it? How *dare* she? She was supposed to be my best friend. Friends didn't do things like that!

I couldn't restrain myself. In full view of several onlookers, I flew at her and grabbed a handful of her hair, pulling it as hard as I could.

She screamed and lashed out at me. Her shoulder bag fell off and books spilled all over the floor. I kicked one of her books and sent it spinning down the corridor.

"Bitch!" she yelled.

"No, you're the bitch!" I shouted back, giving her hair another painful tug as I fended off her flailing arms.

She grabbed my wrists and I let go of her hair. The two of us stood there, panting, glaring at each other like fighting cats. A small knot of people had formed nearby and were all watching avidly.

"Go away, this is private," I yelled at them, but they remained there, staring, hoping we'd start hitting each other again.

"I'm going," Lori muttered, rubbing her wrist where I'd squeezed it.

"Good riddance!" I fired after her.

The group of ghouls dispersed, disappointed that there had been no bloodshed, and I was left on my own, lurking at the end of the corridor, shaking and trying to stifle my sniffs and my tears. I didn't want anyone to think I was a pathetic wimp, but that's exactly what I felt like just then.

I sneaked out of the back door, cut down a lane which was supposed to be out of bounds, walked round the back of the netball pitch, and let myself out of the gate which the caretaker uses to take the rubbish through. I was out on one of the paths which led to the park. It was the long path which wound right to the top of the hill. It was raining and hardly anyone was around. I needed to be on my own, to think, so I continued to walk, even though I was soon soaked through.

How on earth was I going to go back into school this afternoon, and on all the days to come, with my head held high, ignoring the sneers and taunts, knowing that the whole school thought I was a tart? I had no one I could talk to about it – no one at all.

If only Carol-Ann was around, instead of being so far away in London. . .

Somehow, I managed to get through the afternoon just by pinning a permanent "Get lost!" scowl on my face and going into a kind of trance. The only people I felt good about were Mary and Kirsty. They'd helped me. They were nice. They didn't believe the filthy lies.

But they're not lies, prompted my conscience. It was all true. I didn't want to believe it myself. Each time I thought of what I'd done with Sim, or Paul, or Lloyd, I felt sick – so much so that in the end I had to excuse myself from my Shakespeare lesson and make a dash for the toilets, where I found I couldn't be sick because I hadn't eaten anything to be sick with.

I wondered if the teachers knew about the posters. Had they seen them? Even if they hadn't, word must have got back to them, surely? It was a nightmare. I never wanted to go back to school again!

I got home to find Mum out and my brother Ollie sprawled out in front of the TV with a heap of empty lager cans on the carpet. One of his slobby friends was taking up the most comfortable armchair, and as I came in he looked up and gave me a leer.

"You're looking a bit of all right in that school uniform, Rachel. Decidedly kinky!" he said, giving me an exaggerated wink.

I was feeling so hypersensitive about myself and sex that his lecherous remark caused me to explode. "Filthy, disgusting pervert!" I yelled at him. "You're pathetic!"

As I ran out of the room, their drunken laughter followed me.

I pounded up the stairs to my room and closed the door. My bedroom was the only place where I felt safe. I looked longingly at the empty bed which used to be Carol-Ann's. I thought about my life. Nothing mattered any more. Who would care if I lived or died? Was there anyone else, apart from Mum, who really cared about me?

Carol-Ann used to. When we were growing up together, we were closer than close. All at once, a desperate urge to see her came over me. I had some money in my dressing-table drawer, cash I'd been given at Christmas and had never touched. It hadn't made it to the building society because I'd been intending to buy myself something with it. It had sat there for five months.

London was seventy-eight miles away. I remembered hearing Pete say that. I counted my cash. I had thirty-seven pounds. That would be more than enough, surely? The coach would be cheaper, but the train would be quicker.

Before I went, I wrote a note to Mum.

Dear Mum,

I've gone to see Carol-Ann as there are some things I really need to talk to her about. Please don't worry about me. See you later.

Love, Rachel.

I left it on my bed where she'd be sure to find it. Then, making sure I had my sister's address and phone number on me, I crept silently down the stairs.

Chapter 9

About a third of the way into the journey, as I was seriously boiling my lips on a polystyrene mug of watery coffee, I came to my senses and decided I'd gone utterly mad. What was I doing on a train heading for London? I hadn't rung Carol-Ann; I didn't even know if she'd be there. What was I going to do if she wasn't? I didn't know anybody else in London and I hadn't enough money for a hotel. I'd be completely stranded!

Fear curdled the coffee in my stomach and I felt queasy, a condition which wasn't improved by the greasy odour of the cheeseburger the man sitting opposite me was eating. At least he was leaving me alone and not trying to chat or anything.

I'd thought to bring a book with me. I kept trying to read it but the print jumped and danced in front of my eyes and I couldn't make any sense of the words at all, so I gave up and placed it open and face down on the table in front of me. A glance at my watch showed me that I still had just over an hour to go. Then I had the tube journey ahead of me.

Carol-Ann lived in a flat in Camden Town. She'd described it as being almost as good as a house as it was on two floors and had a balcony at the back.

When I got into King's Cross station, I found it was only a short tube journey to Camden Town. I'd never been to London in my life and I felt dreadfully nervous on my own. There were so many people, some of whom looked very sinister indeed: boys with shaven heads dyed orange and clothes with rips in them, and studs in their ears, their eyebrows, their noses – even their lips. In the small town where I lived, people were much more conventional. I'd never seen anyone with a pierced lip or tongue there.

Camden Town station was quite terrifying, full of weirdos and winos. I approached a woman who looked normal and asked her the way to Delancey Street and found it was only a short walk away. As I waited to cross the main road, I was deafened by the roar of traffic. Did quiet streets with pretty houses in them – like my road at home – exist in London? I'd always thought our house was a bit scruffy, but the houses here were filthy and lots of them were covered in scrawls of graffiti. How could Carol-Ann, who loved pretty things and lovely colours, bear to live amongst all this noise and filth and greyness?

"Please be in, please be in!" I repeated to myself as I walked down the busy road towards her house.

There were three bells, so I took a chance and stabbed the top one with my finger. After a short delay, during which I repeated my "Please be in" mantra, a voice squawked down the intercom next to my ear, so loudly that it made me jump.

It was impossible to tell whether the voice was male or female, as the distortion was so bad. "Who's that?" it demanded twice.

"It's – it's Rachel, Carol-Ann's sister. Is she there?" I asked nervously.

"Rachel? *Rachel?* I don't believe it! What are you doing here?" my sister's voice screeched. "Come on up!"

The door buzzed. I pushed it excitedly and nothing happened. I pressed the bell again. "I can't get in," I wailed.

"You've got to push it while it's still buzzing. Look, don't worry, I'll come down and let you in."

As soon as she saw me, I was smothered in hugs and kisses. We hadn't seen each other since Christmas. "She's too busy painting masterpieces to come and visit us," Mum had grumbled.

"Let's have a good look at you," she said. "I've missed you, you know."

"I've missed you, too," I said fervently.

As she held me at arm's length, grinning and gazing at me and laughing about my unkempt hair, which was its normal state of wild frizziness, something struck me about her. She'd put on some weight and it made her look really pretty. She'd always been rather gaunt and angular, her high cheekbones making her cheeks look hollow, like a fashion model. But now . . . well, she looked happy. That was the only word I could find to describe her.

She conducted me into a big, light, airy livingroom with French doors flung open on to a plant-filled balcony. Two electric guitars were hanging on the wall, in the only space not filled with mirrors or Carol-Ann's paintings. One painting was of a handsome black guy with high cheekbones and haunted eyes. He was wearing blue jeans, no shirt, and a red bandanna tied round his head.

"That's Joel," Carol-Ann said.

"Oh. He's gorgeous!" I exclaimed. "Who is he?"

"My boyfriend," she said proudly. "We're living together. He plays in a band. He's a guitarist. He plays jazz. I met him in the Jazz Café round the corner."

I hated jazz, I just didn't understand it, but I didn't tell Carol-Ann. I sat down on a squashy sofa that was draped in exotic purple and red velvet.

"I designed that and had it printed," she said proudly, sitting down opposite me in a wicker chair that was painted in zebra stripes. "Why didn't you ring and say you were coming?" she demanded. "What would have happened if I hadn't been here? And where's Mum? Has she gone shopping, or something?"

Her words were coming out in a rush, piling on top of one another as they always did.

"Shopping? Why?" I queried.

"Thursday's late-night shopping night in Oxford Street," she explained. "I thought you might have come down for that."

"No," I told her. "You know Mum – she never buys anything new. She can't afford it."

"Well, where is she, then? Come on, solve the mystery, for heaven's sake!"

"I'm here on my own," I said. "I've, sort of . . . run away. Mum didn't know I was coming. I've left a note, though. I needed to talk to you. There's no one else who'd understand." I gulped, feeling close to tears.

Carol screwed up her forehead and leant forward in her chair. "This isn't like you, Rachel," she said. "What's happened? You're not pregnant, are you?"

"I hope not!" I said, trying to laugh but only managing a cracked chuckle and a twitch of the mouth muscles.

"What is it, then? You've not caught anything, I hope?"

I shook my head.

My sister's eyes bored into mine as if she were trying to read my mind, but still I hesitated. All of a sudden, faced with my sophisticated sister in wild and wicked London, I feared that she might think my problem was really trivial and that I'd overreacted.

"Come on, Rachel, spit it out. You've come all this way so you've got to tell me," she insisted.

"Promise you won't laugh?" I begged.

"I promise."

"OK, then."

I told her all about it and she listened quietly and intently, as she always had done. At the end of my stumbling account, she rolled her eyes and said, "Talk about feast or famine! Last time we had a heart-to-heart, you weren't going out with anyone, and suddenly you're sleeping with all these blokes! Don't you think you've been over-doing things a bit?"

I looked at her, shocked. I'd thought my sister was more broad-minded than this, and here she was, acting just like Lori or someone. I wished I hadn't come.

I felt myself dissolving into tears. Carol-Ann put her arm round me and gave me a hug.

"I didn't intend to sound like Gran, I was just a bit surprised, that's all. Tell me more about the first boy, Sim. It sounds like he treated you really badly. . ."

We talked for ages, drinking innumerable cups of coffee. Finally, I ran out of words, ending with asking her what she'd have done about the insulting notices.

Being Carol-Ann, she didn't take it nearly as seriously as I had done.

"If it was me, I'd turn it all into a big joke. I'd stick a sign on my classroom door saying *The Brothel – Open For Business*, with a list of prices.

But I'm an extrovert and you're not, so I can't imagine you doing that."

"No!" I admitted, with a watery grin. Trust my sister to manage to turn my worst traumas into fun!

"I think you're best off brazening it out, then. Hold your head high and ignore them all, pretend you're above such childish nonsense," she advised.

I knew it wouldn't be easy. Right now, I felt like leaving school and enrolling in another where they didn't know me and had never heard of my so-called reputation.

"That Lori's a poisonous little cow," she went on. "I never did like her, but she was your best friend so I thought it better not to say anything. Anyway, I might have been wrong about her."

"But you weren't," I pointed out.

"As for that boy Sim, I'd like to punch him in the eye!"

"Or somewhere even more painful," I suggested, and we both laughed.

Then she got serious again. "I'm so sorry your first experience of sex turned out so bad," she said.

Her own first time had been fantastic – she'd told me all about it the day after it had happened, when we were still sharing a bedroom at home.

We talked about her life with Joel for a bit, and then she turned the conversation back to me again. "I think the best thing is to ditch Lori – "

"I already have," I assured her.

– "and make better friends with those two girls who helped you – "

"Mary and Kirsty. I'm doing that already," I assured her.

– "and drop Paul. You've got to be seen to be leading a blameless life. Like a nun. Then, after a while, people will begin to think they must have been completely misled about you and that you're a saint compared to most of the other girls. I think that's the best way to play it. Another coffee? And would you like some biscuits, or a sandwich?"

"Yes, please. I'm starving!" I said eagerly, hearing my stomach rumble. I felt I hadn't eaten for days.

"Maybe it's best if your next boyfriend came from another school. I don't think you can risk going out with anyone else from yours," Carol-Ann said musingly.

I thought about that and decided it made sense. Though I would never have guessed that her advice was more of a prediction. . .

* * *

Talking to my sister had made me feel a lot better. She was so confident and sensible. But I knew that my happier mood would only last for as long as I was with her. If only she could come back home with me and help me through it all — help me face all the cretins and bullies and brain-dead morons who I knew wouldn't give up, but would carry on tormenting me. Once I was back home, I knew the nightmare would start again.

"Don't you think you'd better give Mum a ring?" Carol-Ann said.

My heart started to thump in panic. "She'll be really cross with me," I said. "Anyway, she probably won't be in. I think it's her night for Weightwatchers."

Carol-Ann looked up at the clock on the wall. It was a sunflower with a clock face in the centre. "I think you've just got time to catch a train back if you want to. It'll get you in just before eleven," she said. "I'll come with you to the station. It's only a few stops on the bus."

"I bought a return ticket," I said. "But it seems crazy to rush away so fast when I haven't seen you for ages, or met Joel."

"Then come down for a proper visit soon."

I stood up. Suddenly, all I wanted to do was

get home and avoid any more trouble. If I stayed with Carol-Ann, Mum would be dead worried and I'd miss school tomorrow. Not that I cared about that. But, if I was to take Carol-Ann's advice and beat them, rather than letting them beat me, I'd stroll coolly in there tomorrow as if nothing had happened. At least then, nobody would think I was a wimp!

"You're right as usual," I said, giving my sister a big hug. "Oh, I do wish you were still at home!"

"If I'd stayed at home, I'd never have met Joel. Just wait till you're really in love, then you'll understand," she said.

I gave a hollow laugh. "Me? In love?" I scoffed. "Never in a million years! I'm through with men, I tell you."

She gave a knowing smile. "Just till the next one," she said. "Now, we'd better hurry so you won't miss that train."

I didn't miss it. And Mum didn't miss me. She hadn't even been in my room and seen my note. When I got back, there was a note for me, saying, as I thought, that she'd gone to Weight-watchers with her friend Hilary, whose babysitter was minding the children, and was going to the cinema after that.

103

Huh! What was the world coming to, when mothers did vanishing acts and didn't even realize their daughters were hundreds of miles away? What a relief, though! No angry words, no need for explanations, everything was as it had been before.

If only the world could be as it had been before the "slag" notices, though. At once, anger drummed through my head as I thought viciously of Lori. Was she jealous of me, or what? Had things with Carl got so tame that she envied my freedom to go out with lots of boys? Why didn't she finish with him, if that was the case? Why take it out on me by spreading poison around the school?

School . . . did I really have to go back in tomorrow? Couldn't the place burn down in the night, so I could have a fresh start? Please, oh *please*!

Chapter 10

The school didn't burn down, of course. As I walked in the next day, I felt that everyone was staring at me and pointing and that I was a marked and tainted person. I saw Rosie and Barbie giggling as they looked my way and Barbie made a loud comment along the lines of "Lock up your boyfriends! Look who's here!" So much for thinking Barbie was nicer than the rest of the gang! Actually, they were the Gang of Four now, because Lori seemed to have joined them.

I did what Carol-Ann had recommended and totally ignored them. After lunch, though, I found a really nasty note on my desk. It said, *Warning! This person may have Aids. Don't go near her.*

I burst into tears just as Mrs Bradshaw, who

took our English class for Shakespeare, walked through the door. At once, she strode over to my desk and snatched up the piece of paper.

She read it with a scowl. "What's the meaning of this?" she asked, in the voice she used when detentions were in the air.

I didn't answer. Upset though I was, I couldn't grass on my classmates. I'd have been sent to Coventry for ever if I'd done that.

"It was on your desk, Rachel. Kindly explain it," she insisted.

"It . . . I . . . found it just now when I came in. S-someone left it there," I stammered.

She tore it to shreds and dropped the pieces in the bin. "Aids is a very serious subject. It shouldn't be joked about and used lightly. If I see any more messages like this, I shall take great pleasure in rooting out the culprit," she threatened.

I could see several people staring at Rosie Francks. Lori and Shaz had their heads down, pretending to study their Shakespeare play.

"Now, let's get on with the lesson," she said briskly.

I was left with a great sense of relief. My only hope was that she didn't think *I'd* written it. That would have been the biggest irony of all time.

* * *

I would have been a fool to think things would die down instantly. Sim gave me the filthiest looks imaginable every time we bumped into one another. He'd obviously heard the rumours about me and, from his expression, he clearly agreed with them. It wasn't fair. If anyone was a slag, he was. He was the one who was bonking the older woman, and if I hadn't found out, I might still have been going out with him and I wouldn't have slept with Lloyd and gone so far with Paul. It was he who'd driven me to it by his two-timing.

Paul acted as if he didn't give a damn when I said I didn't want to go out with him again.

"It's your loss, baby," was how he reacted. I wished I'd never been out with him. He was a cold-hearted slimeball, same as Sim.

Life moves in strange twists and turns, doesn't it? I was just beginning to find out that truth for myself. Who would have thought, six months ago, that Lori and I would stop being friends, and that I'd gain two great new ones? Mary and Kirsty seemed glad to welcome a third party into their own friendship.

They both turned out to have a fantastic sense of humour, and we started doing things together after school.

Even with new friends, it still wasn't easy for

me. Rosie and her gang, and Lori, might have felt too scared to pin up any more notices, but they made sure I never forgot that I was a "slag" by hissing the word out of the corner of their mouths whenever they passed me.

One day I opened a textbook to find that one of them had slipped a photograph cut out of a girlie magazine into it. The girl, who was wearing nothing but a bra, stockings and suspenders, looked a teeny bit like me. Rosie (or whoever was responsible) had written my name above it. It was so childish, yet it hurt, just as they had meant it to. My persecution wasn't over.

And then it infiltrated my own home. As I was making my way to the kitchen after school one Tuesday, about a fortnight after that dreadful day, the door of Ollie's room flew open and a cloud of vile cigarette smoke drifted out.

His horrible friend – the one who'd made the creepy remarks about my sexy school uniform – appeared and said, with his worst leer, "Is the brothel open tonight, love? Are there special rates for friends of the family?"

The blood drained from my face. I felt faint. I stared at his horrible face in silence, then I stumbled into the kitchen and slammed the door. Collapsing into a chair, I dropped my head on to my arms and burst out crying.

A few minutes later, Ollie came in.

"Go away!" I screamed at him.

"Sorry about John," he said. "I told him I never want to hear him talking to my sister like that again. He heard about it from his brother in Year Seven, who thought it was all a big joke. I told John that you didn't find it funny at all."

"You're right. It's not funny, Oliver," I said quietly. He knew I only ever called him Oliver when I had something serious to say to him. "You've no idea how terrible it's been for me."

He laid a hand on my shoulder. "You've got to learn to take things in your stride, Sis," he said.

"How?" I raised my tearful eyes to him.

Ollie looked blank. "I dunno. It's a matter of learning to stand up for yourself and fight back, I suppose," he said.

"Fat chance," I mumbled weakly. "But thanks for telling John off for me."

My brother went out, closing the kitchen door behind him to leave me in privacy. Soon after, as I made myself a coffee, I heard loud footsteps and voices, then the bang of the front door as Ollie and his friends went out to the pub. I didn't know where they got the money from. None of them were working. Ollie was twenty-three. It was time he got himself together and did something with his life. If only Mum would chuck him out! And Pete, too — he was just as useless.

Fate must have listened to my prayers because Pete suddenly got a job.

I couldn't believe it. He'd worked in a sports shop when he'd first left school, but he'd left because it was boring and had been on the dole ever since.

When I heard what he was doing, I shrieked with amazement.

"A personal trainer? Like the movie stars have? How did you get to be one of those?"

He gave a smug little smile and flexed his pecs inside his tight black T-shirt. "I've been training down at the gym for ages. I took my instructor's exams and now I'm fully qualified," he said.

"How did you do it without telling us?" I asked him, thinking how Baywatch he looked, with his sunbed tan and his smooth fair hair, which was so like Mum's, whereas I take after frizzy-haired Dad.

It turned out that he'd wanted to surprise us all. He'd been doing lots of sneaky exercise sessions down at the gym.

"You should come down there with me one day, Rachel," he said. "I can get you in free. Come for a swim."

"I'd love that," I told him, never suspecting

what a fatal decision I'd just made.

I went straight from school the very next day. I took a rucksack containing my black Speedo swimsuit, some shower gel and a towel, plus a small bottle of mineral water to wash the taste of chlorine from my mouth.

Before my swim, Pete took me on a tour of the gym equipment, proudly demonstrating everything. As he was my brother, I'd never particularly looked at his body, but now, in his black stretch Lycra gear, I could see that he really had muscles. Not only that, he had several girls eyeing him up.

I told him I'd like a go on the machine that worked your thigh muscles, so he set it up for me, switched on the timer, and left me to it. I could soon get addicted to this, I thought, as I pressed my flab against the weight of the machine.

From there, I progressed to the exercise bike and did ten energetic minutes of pumping pedals. There was a guy on one of the running machines. He was slogging determinedly away, his smooth black hair gleaming in the strong light. He had a good back, broad and strong, and nice legs which weren't too hairy. He looked about twenty or twenty-one.

As he had his back to me, I had a good stare

at him, knowing he couldn't see me. Then the timer pinged and my bike switched off and it was time for my swim.

I love swimming but I don't go nearly often enough. This was marvellous because I had the small pool to myself. I chose a line right up the centre, and swam length after length, varying my strokes. The pool was around a metre and a half in depth all over. There were notices saying No Diving, so I was surprised when the silky surface of the water was suddenly broken by a huge splash and a body went speeding past me underwater.

When the head broke surface, I recognized it as the gleaming black one from the running machine.

"Hi," he said, swimming up alongside me.

"Oh, hi," I replied, trying not to sound too interested though, whether from the exercise or because of him, my heart rate had just speeded up enormously. He was simply gorgeous.

He looked as if he were about to start a conversation. If this had been a few months ago, I would have been happy and flattered that a good-looking boy wanted to talk to me, but now it was the last thing I wanted. I remembered what Carol-Ann had said, that I should give boys a rest for a while, so I swam up to the steps and climbed out of the water without even turning round.

I felt so good after my swim that when Pete asked me to come to the gym again two nights later, I happily agreed. When I saw who was in the swimming-pool ahead of me, my heart sank, though it sank in a very fluttery kind of way. It was that boy again and this time he gave me a wave so there was no way I could pretend I hadn't seen him.

As diving was supposedly not permitted, I held my nose and jumped into the pool. When I surfaced, he was beside me.

"I'm Gary," he said. "You dashed off a bit smartish the other day. I was just going to ask you to have an orange juice with me at the bar later."

The gym did very nice sandwiches and freshly squeezed orange juice, which was delicious.

My mind was at war with my emotions. What could I say to him? I knew I should turn down his invitation, but he was being so nice and friendly that it would have seemed really rude of me. So, very reluctantly, I accepted, knowing there was no way things were going to go any further than the gym bar.

It was three-quarters of an hour before I'd finished my swim, got dry and was walking across the foyer to the bar where Gary was sitting waiting for me.

"Before I say anything else, there's something I must ask you," Gary said.

"What's that?" I asked, as I struggled on to one of the high bar stools.

"Well, I know you've only just started coming here because I'm here nearly every night and I never saw you until the day before yesterday."

"Correct," I responded.

"I saw Pete showing you round. It looked like you two knew each other really well. Is he your boyfriend?"

I burst out laughing. Gary stared at me quizzically.

"No, no, he's just my brother," I gasped when I managed to stop laughing.

Gary pretended to mop his brow. "Phew! Thank heaven for that! So I'm in with a chance, after all," he said.

Oh no, oh no! I thought desperately. Another bloke after my body. What was wrong with me? Did I have Slag tattooed on my forehead?

I must have winced or something, because Gary asked me what was wrong.

"Nothing. Just a touch of cramp. Too much swimming," I lied. "I'm not used to it." That much was true. Between last autumn and now, I'd been almost as much of a slob as Ollie!

We settled into talking. Gary had been a member of the gym since the previous summer. He was dead keen on sports and was in a running team. He hoped to run the London Marathon and had applied for the following year.

Close up, I could see he was a bit younger than I'd thought – nearer my age than twenty. I asked him what he did and he surprised me by saying he was still at school, studying for his A levels. He turned out to be the same age as me, older by just seven weeks. He was taking the same subjects as me, too, which was such a coincidence, it was almost uncanny and made me feel a bit goosebumpy. If I'd been looking for love, I'd have thought we were meant for each other. Soulmates.

Another thing was right about him, too. He didn't go to any of the local schools, but was at the posh public school in Brickenhall, about five miles away.

Carol-Ann's words rang in my ears: *Maybe it's best if your next boyfriend came from another school.*

Firmly, I told myself I was not going to think about a "next boyfriend". Boyfriends were out for the conceivable future. I didn't need them in my life. They'd caused me nothing but heartache and trouble.

Trouble was, as I gazed into Gary's glorious blue eyes and laughed at his jokes, I kept getting this absurd desire to topple off my bar stool and land in his wonderful muscular arms.

I scarcely noticed the time passing but at last he looked at his watch, downed the remains of his third juice and announced that he had to go. I felt a pang of disappointment but I tried hard not to let it show as I glanced at my own watch and said, "I'd better be off, too."

"Would you like a lift anywhere?" he asked me.

He had his own car! Wow! But no thanks. "I – I'm going to Warsley to see a friend." It was lie number two. Just as well we weren't about to begin a relationship, I thought, because this wouldn't have been a good start!

I had to give the gym a miss for several nights after that, because of too much homework, and because I was going out for a pizza with Kirsty and Mary. I'd never dreamt I could be part of a friendship trio, but it was working very well. They lived two streets away from each other and had known each other since primary school. They were almost like sisters. Yet they didn't seem to mind including a third party in their arrangements. It was great fun and helped me not to miss Lori too much. Looking back, she had been quite hard work. Yet it's sad when a friendship breaks up. It's a bit like losing a boyfriend, because there are lots of memories of things you did and said, and reminders – like presents you gave each other.

It was the following Tuesday before I saw Gary again – and what a meeting! Talk about feeling a right wally! I saw him up ahead of me in the gym. When he heard my footsteps on the stairs, he turned, then I missed a step and landed in a heap at the bottom with a twisted ankle.

It was so painful, I had tears in my eyes. Gary descended the stairs two at a time and jumped down to my side. He knelt down and felt my ankle expertly, pronouncing that nothing was broken but I might have pulled a ligament rather than a muscle, and the best thing I could do was put a cold poultice on it straight away, to reduce the swelling.

He went and found Pete for me, and he fetched the first aid box, sprayed my ankle with an anaesthetic spray and bandaged me up. This time, when Gary offered me a lift home, I was in no position to say no.

His car was an untrendy blue Fiesta, but it was clean and in good nick.

"Sorry about the car. My uncle passed it on to me when he bought a new one," he explained. "It was a present when I passed my test last October. One day maybe I'll be able to afford something a bit flashier."

He opened the boot and took out the car stereo and plugged it in. Then he unlocked the glove compartment and revealed a pile of CDs and tapes. He chose one and popped it into the machine. It was a compilation of rock tracks.

"You don't mind this, do you?" he asked, a bit anxiously, as if he thought I was about to judge his whole character from his choice of music.

"No, not at all," I replied. I was quite easy-going about music. I liked almost anything, apart from that kind of twiddly jazz that has no beat, and awful, screeching sopranos singing opera.

Gary started singing along to one of the tracks. His voice was surprisingly good.

"Ever thought of being in a band?" I asked him.

He laughed. "That's everyone's dream, isn't it? No. I can't play an instrument."

"You don't need to if you're the singer," I pointed out.

"I suppose not." He stopped talking to negotiate a tricky junction. Then he went on, "I wouldn't have the nerve to stand up in front of hundreds of people and sing. I'm more of the shy, retiring sort."

"Like me," I said promptly. Then I regretted saying it. I didn't want him to think of me as some colourless little mouse.

He turned his head and gave me a quick grin. Having studied his profile for some minutes, I decided it was flawless. His nose and chin were perfectly in line, his lips – well, just yummy. His black eyebrows could have been sculpted by a famous artist. The vivid blueness of his eyes was quite a shock, contrasted with the jet black sheen of his hair. It made his looks unusual and striking. I thought I had never, ever sat next to such a good-looking boy. I'd once thought Sim was extremely handsome, but his pale, cold, thin-faced looks weren't a patch on Gary.

When we reached my house, he stopped the car and came round to my side to help me out. I leant heavily on his arm as I hobbled in. Mum was in the kitchen, having just got the twins to bed.

"What's happened to you? And who's this young man?" she asked, looking quite anxious.

I explained and she insisted I sit on the sofa

with my foot propped up on a heap of cushions. She offered Gary a cup of tea and he accepted. She chatted to us both for a bit, then said she'd better go and finish the ironing.

That left Gary and me together and I was helpess. If he made a pass or anything, I would be incapable of running away. For a few moments my heart thudded with nervous tension, but I soon began to relax as he chatted about his family, his older brother in America, his father who spent most of his time in London, and his mother who appeared to spend her days playing tennis and going for massages and beauty treatments. It was a different world. My poor mum never got the chance to do things like that. Even if she had the time, she hadn't got the money – though things had improved a little now that Pete was handing over some of his wages for his keep.

Half an hour passed; three-quarters of an hour. Then Gary looked at his watch and stood up.

"Well . . . homework calls, I'm afraid."

"Yes. Me, too," I said.

"No use me saying 'See you down the gym tomorrow,' is it?"

I shook my head ruefully.

"Then how about if I said, 'Let me pick you up and take you out for a Chinese?' "

I stared at him. If I'd thought my heart was beating fast earlier on, now it was going at double that rate!

"You're looking at me as if I'm from the planet Zog! I'm not that awful a prospect to be spending an evening with, am I?" he asked appealingly.

"No, of course not." I gave a nervous laugh. "It's just that . . ." Oh Lord! Lie number three was coming up! ". . . well, I'd made myself a vow of no boyfriends till my mocks were over. I didn't want to be distracted from my work."

Gary came over to me and touched my hair very lightly. "It's so springy!" he said in surprise.

"Bane of my life," I growled.

"It looks great. Wish I had hair that thick. What I was going to say was, I won't distract you from your work, I promise."

I felt numb – paralysed. I couldn't accept, I just couldn't!

Gary reached in his sports bag and withdrew a notepad and a pen. He scribbled his phone number down, tore out the page and handed it to me. "Let me know how your ankle gets on," he said.

After he'd gone, I didn't know whether to laugh or cry. He'd been so good about my lack of enthusiasm for a date with him. He seemed a genuinely nice guy. Oh, if only. . .

Well, it was going to take a week at least for my ankle to start feeling better. That was plenty of time for the situation to cool down. I certainly didn't expect Gary to ring me the following Friday. I hadn't even given him my number!

He'd got it off Pete, of course. Why hadn't I thought of that? He was glad to hear my ankle was feeling a lot better and he mentioned one or two things which might help it heal faster.

"It — it's really kind of you to phone," I said hesitantly.

"I *have* got an ulterior motive," he said. "How about having that Chinese with me tomorrow night?"

This time, I couldn't think of one good reason to say "No".

Chapter 11

As I sat in the Moonlight Chinese Restaurant with Gary, I couldn't help thinking back to my first date with Sim. I'd thought Sim easy to talk to, but Gary was much more so. His conversation was more interesting, too. Sim, I recalled, had talked mostly about himself whereas Gary was more interested in finding out about me and my opinions on things.

From time to time, I deliberately moved my eyes off his face and gazed at the large tropical fish drifting around in the huge tanks lining the walls. I'd been to three Chinese restaurants and they'd all had tropical fish in them. Maybe they ended up on the menu or something. As my eyes followed their meandering movements, I reflected that, although only five months had passed since that first date with Sim, I'd aged years as far as maturity was concerned. I felt I'd been through raging fires and come out safely on the other side, to find myself several steps up on the ladder of character development. With Sim, I'd sat there dumbly, gazing at him with shy, adoring eyes. With Gary, I was giving as good as I got, conversationally, adding to the points he was making, throwing questions back at him about his views on the environment, on student grants, on education.

Naturally, we talked about more trivial things, too. You can't be totally heavy when eating a Chinese with chopsticks! Not when you've got bits of beansprout decorating your lace top where a clumsy flick of a chopstick had deposited them. If I'd been with Sim, I would have been mortified, but with Gary, we just laughed about it.

Some deep instinct told me that I wouldn't have any difficulty with Gary when he took me home. He wouldn't be like the gropy Paul, telling me he was dying from sexual frustration.

He drove me to my door and stopped the car. Then he said I'd better have an early night to rest my ankle, and kissed me softly on the cheek.

"Thanks for a lovely meal, and a lovely evening," I told him.

His smile crinkled his face and made his blue eyes dance. His black hair gleamed in the light of a street lamp.

"Thank *you*! You were the one who made it so special," he said romantically.

In the gloom of the car interior, I could feel myself blushing. Suddenly I found myself wishing he'd kiss me properly, but instead, he got out to help me out.

He offered me his hand. As I stood up from the passenger seat, the suspension bounced me towards him and, laughing, he caught me in his arms. His mouth met mine in a soft, sweet kiss. He was so gentle. He kissed my lips as if they were as fragile as butterflies' wings. He kissed me as if I'd break if he pressed too hard. And all the time his arms didn't stir from the small of my back, as if they'd been glued in place.

It was the first undemanding, tender kiss any boy had given me. It was a kiss that respected the fact that I was me.

"Good-night, Rachel," he said softly, releasing me at last. "See you soon."

And then he was gone, driving off into the night, leaving me trembling on the doorstep with my lips still tingling and my heart alight.

I got in to find the kitchen alive with classical music and Mum sitting there over a cup of coffee with a dreamy expression on her face. She seemed in a similar mood to me.

"Had a good time, love?" she asked me.

I told her about my date, and then she told me she'd been out on one, too! She'd mentioned Ken a few times. He was a widower of about fifty, who worked in her office. I'd no idea they were keen on one another. Apparently they'd been to a piano recital at the town hall and Ken had bought her a cassette by the string quartet that had been playing, which was what she was listening to now.

It was the first time in ages that I'd felt so close to Mum. It was good to be able to swap notes about boyfriends. I was really pleased for her and said I'd love to meet Ken. She said it was best to wait and see how things went.

"I don't want to introduce him to Ollie too soon — he might go off me!" she joked.

One thing she said about Ken rang a bell with me, and that was the fact that he made her laugh. It was the same with Gary. Things were always fun with him, as I gradually found out during May.

I felt relaxed with him because, unlike the others, he wasn't putting me under any pressure to have sex with him. In fact, we hadn't even discussed it. We necked, we hugged, and that was it – and it was enough for me.

It wasn't that I didn't have any desire to throw myself at him. Of course I did! But, for the first time ever, the word "respect" had entered my vocabulary. I respected him because he made it obvious that he respected me.

With no hassles about sex, we just enjoyed each other's company, going for drives, walks, to his school cricket match, to rock groups in pubs, to parties. It was all stuff I loved doing, and he was the best person in the world to do it with. I was proud to be seen out with him because, even when he was in jeans and trainers and a T-shirt, he always looked so neat and gorgeous.

I felt I was the luckiest girl alive. Sometimes, I speculated about what might have happened to me if Gary hadn't appeared on the scene. Would I have stuck to my resolution to steer clear of boyfriends? Would I have become the class swot, which was the title poor Mary used to have before a new boy called Chris Smither took it over? Who knows!

I only knew that I was happy with the way things had turned out. It was summer, I was in love, and all the things that had gone wrong in my life were fading, becoming less hurtful as time went on.

Even Rosie & Co. had ceased to worry me.

When Rosie had made one of her "slag" remarks recently, I just threw it back at her and said that it took one to know one.

As for Lori, she tried to come crawling back and apologize but I told her to get lost. What a cheek! I thought. Maybe she was jealous at seeing me going round with Mary and Kirsty. Maybe she missed my marvellous company (ha ha!). Whatever she wanted of me, she couldn't have it. She'd blown it. For ever.

I'd been dying for half-term to come round. A whole week to spend with Gary! Wow! While we were out one night, I suggested to him that we take a boat out on the river that week. I was quite good at rowing. Dad had taught me during a holiday in Wales when I was eleven.

When Gary said he wouldn't be around as he had to go to Somerset with his parents for the half-term break, I felt as though someone had stolen the ground from under my feet. I felt wobbly, uncertain, unable to exist without him. What would I do for a whole week?

Oh Gary, Gary! I thought yearningly that night. *How am I going to exist without you?* The week loomed ahead like an entire year. If I didn't fill it up with something, I'd go crazy.

What I did was to visit Carol-Ann – with Ollie,

of all people. He was going for a job interview in London (yes, really!) and he drove me down. He slept on the sofa for two nights and I curled up on some big cushions. Then he went home and I stayed another two nights and had the sofa all to myself.

I had a fantastic time, going to London Zoo, to Camden Market, to clubs and art exhibitions. Joel and Carol-Ann took me out to China Jazz for a meal. The band playing that night were friends of Joel's. They were brilliant and we all stayed up ever so late, because some of the musicians came back to the flat afterwards for a drink. How I envied my sister and her boyfriend their relaxed lifestyle and their freedom to live together!

When I was Carol-Ann's age, in two years' time, maybe I'd be living with Gary! The thought was wild. It was wicked. I loved it and yearned for it. To live with him – to share a bed with him every night!

Suddenly, the parts of me that had ceased to work since Sim shot shockingly back to life. I wanted Gary, but I knew I mustn't think this way or I might go and spoil things. I tried to ignore the sensations in my body, though it was difficult, especially when I had dreamed about him, as I often did.

When I got home on Thursday – Gary wasn't due back till Sunday, worse luck! – there was a letter waiting for me, postmarked Shepton Mallet. I could hardly open the envelope, I was shaking so much. Had he had second thoughts and decided he didn't want to see me when he got back? Had he met somebody else down there?

It took all the courage I had to open the letter – and when I did, the first words I saw were, *All my love, Gary*, so I knew that everything must be all right.

After that, I unfolded the four pages and savoured every word on them.

People say that men aren't much good at expressing their emotions and that women are much better. There was no way I could have written the things Gary wrote. I wouldn't have had the guts. And even though English was my best subject, I don't think I could have expressed myself half as well as he did. He poured out his heart on to the page, line after line about how he felt, what he thought of me. How he'd like to kiss me delicately from the top of my head to the tips of my toes. . . How he'd like to walk naked in the sea with me at sunset. . . How his love for me was driving him out of his mind. He said he'd never felt this way about anyone before and he hoped I felt the same about him.

After I'd finished reading, I cried. Then I kissed his name on the last page. Then I read it all again. I'd never felt so happy in my life. This was the magic I needed to drive all the horror away. Secure in the knowledge that Gary really loved me, I could laugh at the pathetic attempts of Rosie & Co. to upset me. I could even sneer at Sim. Maybe his air stewardess had flown off to Hawaii with a millionaire from Business Class and ditched him. I hoped so!

There was one particular bit in Gary's love letter that I read time and time again. I kept returning to it because I didn't quite know what to think.

When I get back, he wrote, *there's something very special I want to ask you. I don't know how you'll react. It depends on whether, like me, you feel we've reached the stage in our relationship where we should take it to a deeper level.*

I puzzled and puzzled about what he meant. Then, on the Sunday evening when he got back, I found out. . .

Chapter 12

Gary came round and picked me up in the car.

"I cleaned it in your honour. Look!" he said, indicating the gleaming paintwork and spotless interior. Even the mirrors sparkled.

We drove off and as soon as we got to the end of my road, he stopped the car.

"I can't wait another second," he said. "Come here!" And he enveloped me in his arms and gave me a dizzying kiss.

"Whew!" I said when I surfaced.

"There's lots more where that came from," he promised.

He took me to a Greek restaurant, where we had kebabs and I had a very large glass of white wine which made me feel even dizzier than his kiss had done.

After we'd given the waiter our order, he said, a bit anxiously, "You did get my letter, didn't you?"

"Yes, I did." My reply was quiet and, I hoped, full of meaning as I gazed into his eyes, trying to convey how much I adored him. Because I did. I thought about him day and night.

In boring moments during lessons, I kept conjuring up his vivid blue eyes, like pieces of the sky in midsummer, and that gleaming black hair, and the set of his lips and cheekbones, and the way his face crinkled into two curvy lines at the corners of his lips whenever he smiled.

Right now, his skin was tanned from his holiday. He looked edibly gorgeous. I could have licked him like an ice-cream.

"What did you think?" he pressed me.

"What do you mean?" I enquired.

"You look pretty when you pout like that." He laughed and wiggled his eyebrows. Then he said, "I wonder what you look like when you're angry?"

"I don't often get angry, but I hope you'll never have to find out," I said. "Anyway, about your letter – I loved it. I can't count how many times I've read it. Thank you for writing it. I think you're very brave."

133

"Does that mean I'm never likely to get a love letter from you?" he asked.

"Of course not! It's just that I couldn't have written the first one." I was blushing. I could feel it. I looked down at my plate, then up again into his eyes.

He reached across the tablecloth and took hold of my left hand, which was toying with my red paper napkin, red to match the cloth no doubt. The candle that flickered in its glass holder was scarlet, too. Red for love . . . and for danger.

"I love you, Rachel. It's true. Do you love me?" His voice was low and husky. A shiver ran right through me.

"Yes," I replied.

"Then let me hear you say it."

"I love you, Gary."

As the words left my lips, everything in the room seemed to swirl. I felt I'd never said anything as important as this before. It was a landmark in my life.

To be interrupted by a waiter just then was the worst thing that could have happened. I could have cried. Yet, as I tucked my feelings back inside my heart and my napkin into my belt, I reflected that maybe it was good not to be quite so intense for a while. If we'd continued like that, I couldn't have eaten a thing.

134

Gary was driving, so he wasn't drinking. When I finished my wine and let out an uncontrollable hiccup, he laughed. During the main course, he'd chatted about his holiday. We'd ordered dessert – delicious, syrupy Greek cakes. I finished the final crumb of mine, dabbed my sticky lips and leaned back in my chair with a big, fat, bloated sigh.

"Enjoy it?" he asked.

"Oh, yes!" I assured him.

"Happy?"

"Yes, of course," I said.

"It's my treat tonight," he announced.

Even though I was a bit drunk, I could sense that the atmosphere between us had changed. Gary looked nervous. He was twisting his paper napkin in his hands, screwing it up, then unfolding it.

"Rachel. . ." He paused.

I looked at him, frowning slightly. "Yes?"

He glanced away, then back at me. Then he said, "Remember what I said in my letter, about getting our relationship on to the next stage?"

I bit my lip, my heart thudding nervously, and nodded.

"Did you realize what I was getting at?"

"I . . . er . . . don't know," I faltered, feeling in a complete daze. I was glad we were in a private corner, where no one could see my face, or overhear what we were saying.

He reached for my hand again. "I'm sure you do. What I'm trying to say, Rachel, is that I want you more than I've ever wanted any other girl. I love you, I love kissing you, holding you, but it isn't enough. I want more."

His blue eyes blazed into mine.

"I think you know what I'm talking about. Surely you must feel it, too? It's getting so frustrating, not having anywhere to take you where we can be alone . . . where we can make love . . . That's what I want. Don't you?"

My hand flew to my mouth and before I could stop myself, I'd gasped, "Oh, no!"

Gary looked stricken. "Oh. Have I overstepped the mark? I'm sorry if I've offended you, Rachel. I honestly thought you felt as much for me as I felt for you. I fancy you like crazy. I thought you felt the same. . ."

He looked down at the table, his cheekbones reddening slightly. I released my hand from beneath his, then gently stroked the back of his hand and gave it a squeeze. We've been going out for nearly three months, I thought. I slept with Lloyd on the fifth date, I slept with Paul – well, all but! – on the first and I didn't love either of them. So what was holding me back from letting the boy I loved, who loved me, make love to me? Was it because I feared he wouldn't respect me if I gave in?

I knew I had to say something to relieve his tense confusion.

"Don't worry, Gary, you haven't said the wrong thing. It was just a bit of a shock, that's all. I wasn't expecting it," I said. "Of *course* I fancy you – more than anyone I've ever met! And – and I *do* want us to make love. I just don't want you to think that I'm. . ."

I couldn't get the word out. Gary was staring at me. "What are you worried that I'd think?" he prompted.

"That I'm a s-slag." I stumbled over the word. It was the word I hated most in the English language.

Gary gave me such a tender, loving look that I almost dissolved. "I'd never think that of you, Rachel," he said.

Oh Gary, if you only knew! I thought agonizedly.

"I keep thinking of lying next to you, holding you in my arms," he said softly, musingly, his eyes developing a faraway look. "When it happens, I want it to be perfect. All the circumstances have got to be right.

"I'd like us to be in a big bed with satin sheets.

137

There'd be a bottle of champagne in an ice bucket. We'd have smoked salmon and strawberries to eat if we got hungry. And, best of all, we'd have to have all night together. I don't want our first time to be some sordid grapple in a shop doorway, or all cramped up in the car."

I thought of Paul and Lloyd. It was just as if Gary had probed my mind! Banishing the guilty memories, I said, "But we'll never get all that! Satin sheets? Champagne?"

He laughed. "Probably not. But I can dream, can't I?"

He called the waiter over and paid the bill. He wouldn't even let me contribute to the tip.

As we walked hand in hand towards the car, Gary said, "Rachel, I meant it when I said I've never felt this way about anyone before. I love you and I want you."

He drew me into his arms and I trembled against him. He stroked my hair, then nuzzled his lips into it.

"Beautiful hair. . ." he murmured into my awful frizz.

Then he said, "If I could arrange it, what would you say?"

"Do you mean my hair?" I joked, hoping he'd forgive me, knowing I had to play for time. If I said "yes" right away, he might think badly of me. I wasn't going to throw myself at him. Gary was worth waiting for.

"No, I jolly well don't mean your hair! You know what I mean," he said. His lips moved down from my hair to my cheek, then found my lips. We stood there next to his car, lost in a kiss.

"I think you're a bit shy. Are you, Rachel?" he asked me.

"Mm," I confirmed.

"I thought so. You're a really sweet girl, do you know that? I hate forward girls. I don't think you've ever been propositioned like this before, have you?"

I had to lie — I *had* to! I had to make Gary think I was a virgin otherwise he might lose respect for me. So I shook my head and said, "No, I haven't."

He separated from me and unlocked the car. I got in in my usual clumsy way, banging bits of me on the roof and the dashboard. Then I slammed the door too hard, so that the whole car jerked.

"Oops! Sorry," I apologized.

"I've made you nervous, haven't I?" He gave a light laugh. "It's me who should be apologizing for being a normal, randy bloke! Forgive me?"

"Of course I do," I said.

139

"Love me?"

"Yep."

"How much?" His blue eyes were staring at mine. I could almost see his feelings pulsating through them in waves of energy.

"Lots," I murmured. My tummy was doing backflips. There was a big butterfly in my chest where my heart used to be. "Lots and lots," I added.

His hand sneaked over my shoulders and caressed the back of my neck in a way which made me shiver all over.

"I've never been out with anyone like you. You're so natural, so feminine. I hate loud, butch women. Promise you'll stay just the way you are now?"

"I'll try," I replied, but the voice of my conscience was saying, *What if he finds out the truth? If he finds out I'm not a virgin, I'll just die!*

Then I had an even worse thought than that. If I slept with him, he'd be bound to find out I wasn't one. That meant I couldn't make love with Gary ever. I had to keep on saying no. Sooner or later, he'd get fed up and finish with me and I'd lose the only boy I'd ever truly loved – and it would be all my stupid fault!

Next day, looking for something to distract my

mind from my mega problem, I bought a magazine and found an article in it entitled, *Can He Tell If You're A Virgin?*

Nothing could have been timelier and I read it avidly. It said that, if a girl had used tampons and led an active life with lots of cycling, horse-riding and activities like that, then she was unlikely to bleed when she first had sex as the hymen, which was the membrane that stretched across the entrance to the vagina, would have been broken already. What a relief!

However, just as I was beginning to stop worrying, the thought occurred to me that Gary mightn't know this. I could hardly cart the magazine around with me everywhere until we made love, and leave it open on the bed at the appropriate page, could I?

"Fat lot of use you are!" I shouted at the magazine and hurled it into the waste-paper basket in my bedroom. It was too heavy and knocked the wicker basket over and all sorts of yukky rubbish like old apple cores and bits of cotton wool with mascara on them fell all over the carpet.

Next day my period started and I broke out in a load of horrible spots. I hoped against hope that this wasn't the night that Gary intended to seduce me. It would be just my luck! I didn't even want him to see me, looking like this. We had a date, too.

He was so nice that he pretended not to notice my spots. I'd made great efforts with my hair, but the gel I'd put on had made it look greasy rather than shiny. I was an absolute disaster but still Gary said, "You look nice tonight, Rachel," when he picked me up.

There was an open air rock concert on locally and Gary had bought tickets. I'd insisted on giving him the money for mine but he wouldn't agree to take it till I pointed out that he could look on it as a contribution towards petrol for all the lifts he'd given me.

It was a cool evening with a bit of a breeze and I turned up the collar of my denim jacket. I got so wrapped up in the music that I suddenly realized I'd got really chilly because I hadn't moved for ages. I shivered and at once Gary put his arm round me and drew me to him.

I closed my eyes and rested my head against his shoulder.

"We'll go if you're too cold," he said.

"I don't want to go, I'm enjoying it. I'll be OK as long as you keep your arm round me," I told him.

"Snuggle up, then," he said, brushing my forehead with his lips, which must have taken some courage on his part as there was a huge, pulsating spot right in the middle of it.

Then he kissed me on the tip of my nose and suddenly we were face to face, kissing properly, and my chilliness had turned into a burning heat as I felt his body pressed tightly against mine.

I don't know how long we kissed, but in the end we sensed movement all around us and realized that the concert was over and people were going home.

Gary laughed. "I think the world could have ended just then and we wouldn't have noticed," he said.

"It's always like that when you kiss me," I told him, tracing the shape of one of his black eyebrows with my finger.

He replied by kissing his fingers, then brushing the kiss on to my lips with them. I pretended to nibble his fingers and he laughed again. "Love you," he said.

"Spots and all?" I challenged him.

"Yeah, spots and all. What spots?" he replied.

I pointed. "This one here . . . and this one here. . ."

"I hadn't noticed. But, now you come to mention it, there is something resembling Vesuvius erupting in the middle of your forehead," he said gravely.

"Pig!" I squeaked. Then I said, "Oh look, you've got a spot, too!" I'd found one, right on the point of his jaw.

He felt it. "That's a bite. A blasted gnat or something's got me."

"Well, at least it didn't get you on the end of your nose, so count yourself lucky," I said.

"It got you, though," he said.

My hand flew to my nose but there was nothing there, so I hit him playfully, tucked my arm in his and we followed the crowd over the field, back to civilization. I felt like skipping, I was so happy. I was in a proper relationship, with a boy who really loved me. We could laugh, joke with one another, tease and not get hurt. It was just brilliant. Fancy having a boyfriend you could even joke about spots with! I loved him so much.

Yet, despite our relaxed, loving relationship, I still felt nervous about the looming prospect of sex – I, Rachel, who had let one boy seduce me far too easily and had thrown myself at two more! Gary was too important to me. I was terrified of messing things up. In a way, much as I loved and fancied him, I thought I'd rather we didn't make love at all. Yet I knew that, between two people who loved each other as much as we did, sex was inevitable sooner or later. . .

Chapter 13

Three weeks later, it happened. This time, there was no sneaking about, no having to lie to Mum. It was a baking hot Wednesday in July, just after school had broken up. I should have been looking for a job, but the weather was just too beautiful and Gary thought the same.

"Come on, let's go for a run in the country," he said.

By now, Gary was often at our house, because Pete was working most of the time and Ollie – three cheers! – had got the job in London and had moved out in June.

Mum adored Gary. "Much nicer than that Sim fellow you brought home. I don't know why, but I thought there was something sneaky about him," she said. She was dead right, though I didn't tell her.

As soon as she heard we were going off into the countryside, she decided to pack us a picnic.

"You needn't have bothered, Mrs Kelly, we would have found somewhere cheap to eat," Gary said.

"In summer, with the place crawling with tourists? You'd be lucky!" she said darkly.

Gary was looking utterly yummy that day, in a snow white T-shirt and jeans shorts. I had on plain black shorts and a red sleeveless vest. Round my neck I wore some red and black beads on a leather thong. Carol-Ann had painted them and made them into a necklace for me as part of my birthday present.

When he steered off the main road and down a series of ever smaller ones, I began to grow curious. He seemed to know this obscure route very well.

"Where are we going?" I asked.

"You'll see," was all he'd tell me.

I put my hand on his knee and gave it a gentle squeeze.

"Careful! I can't drive straight when you do that," he said.

I removed my hand reluctantly because I had an urge for constant physical contact with Gary,

146

even if it was just his sleeve against my arm.

When I saw the small white cottage set amongst a clump of dark conifers, it never dawned on me that that could be our destination. I was amazed when he turned off down the stony track which led to the front door.

"Where are we? What are we doing here?" I questioned him.

He grinned, produced a bunch of keys and started turning them in locks. Then he ushered me in with a flourish.

"No one will disturb us here," he said.

"But—"

"Ssh!" He silenced my worries with a kiss. "It's my parents' cottage," he explained. "I said we were going for a run in the country so they asked if I'd drop in and just check that the place was OK. So here we are!"

He took me on a tour of the old cottage. Its ceilings were so low that he had to duck in places. The kitchen at the back looked out on to a lovely garden, full of flowers.

"There's an old man in the village who looks after the garden for us," he said.

"He's made a great job of it," I commented.

Then we went upstairs. There was a tiny bathroom and two bedrooms. The front one was a bit dark, but the back one, a long room overlooking the garden, was filled with sunlight. Particles of dust danced in the sunbeams like glittery mist. The old carved bed was adorned with a patch-work quilt in squares of red, pink and blue.

"My grandmother made that," Gary said.

We fell silent. At first, I was drinking in the atmosphere. Then I became aware of a tingling tension in the air. Gary was staring at me. I felt anchored to the wooden floor, unable to move. As if in slow motion, he moved towards me and then, hardly noticing how I got there, we were lying on the quilt together and Gary was stroking my hair.

"Rachel . . . oh Rachel, I want you so much," he said, his voice a low, throbbing moan.

We clung to each other, our mouths clamped together. Both of us were trembling. This was it, I knew it was, and I wanted it to happen. My body was doing things I'd never felt it do before, as if every cell was crying out for Gary's touch.

Very gently, he lifted up my T-shirt, kissing each bit of my body that he revealed. I wasn't wearing a bra and when he kissed my breasts, I felt electric shocks and shivers zap through my flesh.

He ripped his own T-shirt off and I kissed every bit of his smooth, warm chest. There was something about the shape of his shoulders that

148

drew my lips to them. I couldn't stop kissing them and stroking them. His skin tasted salty and delicious.

He lifted one of my hands to his lips and gently sucked my middle finger into his mouth. I did the same to his. There we were, our bodies joined by our fingers. It was like a metaphor for that much more important joining together, which my mind was still trying to resist. Only the rational, logical side of my brain was slipping away, overpowered by the rush of magical physical sensations caused by Gary's lips and fingers, and the feel of his firm, warm, lithe body against mine.

"Oh Gary, oh Gary!" I sighed, as my body surrendered at last to his.

"Rachel!" he groaned, as we became one.

Then time stopped and my brain stopped and there was nothing except increasingly blissful physical sensation. Something was happening to me. A wonderful warm feeling was forming deep in the core of me and spreading out in waves. It was taking me over.

"Gary, Gary!" I cried, pulling him tightly against me. "I love you, Gary!"

"I love you, too." His lips met mine and it was like drowning together, sinking through layers of love, and pleasure, and warmth, and utter, utter joy.

"You're crying," he said wonderingly, touching my wet face.

"I . . . I love you," I told him, my voice shaking like my body. "I'm so happy."

"I love you, too. Oh God, Rachel, that was wonderful!" he said. "Are you all right?"

I assured him that I was. Only then did I realize that I hadn't thought about Sim, or Paul, or Lloyd. Gary had managed to perform the miracle I wanted, and had driven them out of my mind. I felt as if this had been my true first time, the real loss of my virginity, lost with a boy I loved beyond belief, who had awoken my numbed feelings and made me come alive again.

We stayed in the bedroom all afternoon, until the sun had left the garden and its last rays were filtering through the trees. By that time we had got to know every inch of one another's bodies. Gary had touched and stroked me everywhere and I'd never known that caresses could feel so utterly exquisite. When I stroked his back gently, my palm scarcely brushing his skin, he shivered all over and said it was ecstasy. And when he kissed my toes, and all the way up my legs, I closed my eyes and groaned, feeling every tiny nerve-ending respond, all over the surface of my body.

At last, extremely belatedly, we ate our picnic, tearing at the sandwiches like ravening wolves and gulping down our drinks. I'd never been so thirsty before, never appreciated food and drink so much. Mum's cheese and pickle sandwiches tasted better than any gourmet meal at a five-star restaurant.

Gary was rather quiet as we drove home, but I didn't start wondering about it. I was half asleep and knew he must be tired out, too.

Before he dropped me off, he said, "Thank you for the most wonderful day of my life. I'll never forget it as long as I live."

"Neither will I," I assured him, with all the emotion I could muster. When we kissed good-bye, we kissed with the full knowledge of each other's bodies. I felt I'd grown up at last and that Gary, in this one short day, had turned me from a girl into a woman. Now I knew how sex should feel, and it was bliss, the best thing in the world.

When I rang my sister and told her all about it, Carol-Ann chuckled and said, "Welcome to the real world, sister!" She said she was really glad for me and that she hoped she'd meet Gary soon.

He had things to do the next day, but I was so tired that I spent half of it in bed, recovering, and the rest of it babysitting so that Mum could go out with Ken.

It was strangely silent in our house, with Ollie away in London and Pete at work at the gym. Ollie had taken most of his stuff off to his new flat – he was sharing a house with four other people – and the back room which had been his was now open for use by the general household again. I'd forgotten what a nice room it was, with its windows overlooking the garden.

The twins and I played in the garden. I filled their inflatable paddling pool for them and they squealed with glee as they jumped in and out of the water and played with rubber toys.

After I'd fed them and got them off to bed, I sat and watched some TV, then started idly flicking through a pile of magazines Mum had left in the lounge. One of them turned out to be a mail order catalogue. It had pages of jewellery in the back and I played the game of, "If I could afford to buy anything on these pages, what would I have?"

Having picked myself a sapphire bracelet and a ruby and diamond ring, I then found myself in the men's section. There, in pride of place on the page, was a fantastic gold chain, not too chunky and macho, more stylish and elegant. I could just imagine it gleaming on Gary's suntanned chest and, the more I thought about it, the greater was the urge to buy it for him.

It wasn't his birthday, though. Would he accept it, as a love token maybe, like the locket which Sim had given me and I'd thrown back at him?

I had a quick shudder as I thought about Sim, and instantly banished him from my mind. Creep! Ugh! Thank heavens he'd left school now and I'd never see him again!

The chain was a lot of money, more than I could afford, but it was possible to pay in instalments. When I got a holiday job – and I knew I'd better start looking – I'd be able to pay them with no difficulty and till then, my own savings were enough to fund the deposit and the first month's payment.

With a big, happy smile on my face, I wrote off for the chain. I didn't dare use the proper order form as it had Mum's customer number on and I didn't want her to know I was doing it, so I just sent a letter explaining that I was ordering it from my mother's catalogue but it had to be sent to me personally. It did say you had to be over eighteen to place an order, but I ignored that. How would they ever know?

Gary and I met again on Friday. My heart

leaped with the sheer joy of seeing him and, from the look in his eyes, he felt the same about me. I recalled the words in his letter about taking our relationship to a deeper level. It had certainly worked. My love for him had both deepened and strengthened. He was everything to me now. I couldn't imagine ever wanting to go out with another boy. I certainly didn't want to make love with anyone else. The thought was positively repulsive!

We couldn't make love again because there was nowhere for us to go. Relatives of Gary's were staying in the cottage for the next month, so we couldn't go back there, but I felt we might be able to organize something one night when Mum was going out with Ken.

I didn't feel desperate about it because it was worth waiting for. Gary told me he felt the same and he'd wait six months if necessary, because he had the memories of that day in the cottage to carry him through. My heart sang when he said that, as it meant he wasn't putting any time limit on our relationship and, as far as he was concerned, we'd still be going out in six months' time. I instantly felt more relaxed about things. I'd been a bit worried that he might get bored with me, but now it seemed that the thought had never entered his head. I felt well and truly loved.

On Saturday night, he'd been invited to a party and he asked me to go with him. We went out for a pizza first. He was looking great, in grey chinos and a rock band T-shirt. I was wearing my favourite short, red, strappy dress. He had the car so he wasn't drinking. I decided I'd have just one glass of wine, then go on to mineral water. I'd seen too many of my friends make idiots of themselves when they were drunk, and I didn't want to join them. Lori had been sick all down the stairs at a party once. It wasn't a pretty sight and I'd had to help clean her up and get her home. I never wanted to get in a state like that myself.

When we walked into the house where the party was being held, I felt a bit shy because there wasn't anyone there I knew. Gary introduced me to several friends of his and I made polite conversation, but I was glad when he decided to stop talking and dance with me.

Enclosed in his arms, I dreamily cradled my head against his shoulder and let my feet follow his. But all at once, the bubble of love and warmth that I'd been floating in was shattered by a hard, sneery voice which I knew only too well.

It was Sim's voice, and the words he spoke made me feel sick with anxiety. "Oh, look!" he exclaimed. "If it isn't the scarlet woman herself!

Hello, Rachel. Notching up another score, I see."

I spun round and glared at him. "Get lost, slimeball!" I hurled at him.

With a curl of his lip, he went off to the kitchen to get a drink.

"Who was that?" Gary enquired icily. "Why did he talk to you like that?"

So he'd noticed, after all. I'd hoped he was too lost in the music to catch Sim's words.

"He's my ex-boyfriend. We finished ages ago. It was his fault we broke up," I said, though I didn't tell him about the air stewardess in case he thought Sim and I had had a sexual relationship, too. I had to keep my murky past from Gary at all costs. Thank God I was wearing a red dress, which would explain the "scarlet woman" remark!

After the encounter with Sim, the party was ruined for me and I told Gary I wanted to go home.

"But it's far too early. It's not even midnight yet," he protested.

"I've got a bad headache. I think it's the heat," I lied.

When I said that, Gary was very sympathetic and drove me back at once.

"I'm really sorry about spoiling things for you," I said, giving him a soft kiss on the cheek.

"It doesn't matter," he said. Then he paused. "It was that bloke, wasn't it? That's what upset you."

"No, of course not! I wouldn't let a dork like him get to me," I bluffed, but I could see that Gary wasn't altogether convinced. It was something in the way he compressed his lips and stared into the distance, instead of into my eyes.

Maybe it was in order to sort Sim out and stop him upsetting me again that Gary went back to the party. . .

Chapter 14

I didn't find out for several days that Gary had gone back there, and I found out in the most awful way. I didn't hear from him the day after the party, but I wasn't surprised because he'd mentioned that his grandparents were visiting. But when I didn't hear from him on the Monday either, I began to worry.

Eventually, at five o'clock, I rang him and when he answered, he sounded really peculiar. Sort of off-hand.

"Oh, it's you. Hello," he said. There was no affection in his voice. He might have been talking to someone from school who he didn't particularly like.

His tone threw me so much that I couldn't think what to say. Normally, I didn't need a reason for phoning because he always sounded so pleased to hear from me, and then we'd rattle on, telling each other about things we'd been doing.

"I . . . er . . . I just wondered if you got back from the party all right," I said lamely.

"I must have done. I'm here, aren't I?" he said, still sounding cold and weird.

My heart started thumping uncomfortably and, despite the warm weather, my hands grew cold. "I – I thought I'd let you know Mum's going out tomorrow night," I told him. I knew he was waiting for this. Surely he'd sound pleased?

"So what?"

I couldn't believe I'd heard him say it. "Well, I thought we could . . . you know. . ."

"I know what you mean." He still sounded weird. There wasn't a trace of warmth or humour in his voice.

Frantic, I began to babble. "Gary? What's wrong? Something is, I can tell. Please tell me what it is. Is there anything I can do? I love you, Gary. I've missed you."

There was a silence. Then he said, "I thought you'd have guessed what was wrong."

"Well, I haven't, so suppose you tell me." It was my turn to sound cold now. He was deliberately withholding something from me and it was very unfair of him.

"OK, I will tell you. But not now. Not over the phone," he said.

"Come round to my house tomorrow, then. Come around eight," I said.

For the rest of that day and far into the night I worried and fretted. I knew I wouldn't relax till I saw him and had an explanation.

When at last I opened the door to him that Tuesday evening, I saw at a glance that he'd changed. His face was set and hard. Despite my enthusiastic, welcoming smile, he didn't smile back and he avoided my eyes and actually turned his head away when I tried to kiss his lips.

Tears sprang to my eyes and I led him blindly into the lounge, stumbling over the strip of metal in the doorway that held the carpet down and bashing my leg on the edge of the sofa.

"Ouch!" I exclaimed, falling on to the sofa and rubbing my leg.

If I'd expected sympathy, none was forthcoming. He didn't even sit on the sofa next to me, but chose a chair some distance away.

There were two routes I could follow, I realized, my mind in overdrive. One was more tears, the other was anger. I chose anger, because I felt I was totally in the clear, as I hadn't done anything wrong.

"Right," I snapped. "Just what is this all about?"

I folded my arms and waited.

"You haven't been honest with me, Rachel."

"Yes, I have!" I cried defiantly. "I don't know what you mean!"

"All that stuff about being shy and virginal. What a laugh!" His mouth twisted ironically and a cold shudder ran right through me. "What kind of a dumb idiot did you think I was? Did you honestly think I wouldn't find out what a slag you were, sooner or later?"

"How dare you call me that!" I yelled hoarsely, hating the torrents of tears that poured down my face.

"Call you what? *Slag?* But it's true, everyone says so. Rachel Kelly, the tart of Meadowbank School. Slaggy Kelly, who's been had by half the boys there. The other half were either too young or didn't fancy you. And I thought you were so sweet, so inexperienced. . ."

His voice dried up. He turned his face away. I saw his throat jerk and a quiver cross his face, and for a moment I thought he was crying, too.

Then he turned back to me. "You've played a fine game with me, haven't you? I bet I was only one of a string of boys you were seeing. How many were you sleeping with?"

"None! There weren't any. Only you," I gasped. "And I haven't – I didn't – there was only Sim—"

"And the rest!" he scoffed, not allowing me to finish.

Despite the searing agony in my heart, I took a deep breath and said, in a calm, steady voice, "Surely it's only fair to tell me who told you this?"

"I went back to the party as it was early and some of my mates hadn't arrived yet. I saw that Sim of yours and decided to do a bit of probing to find out what really happened between you. He said that you seduced him, then you dumped him and started sleeping your way through the rest of the school. Two of your friends from school confirmed it."

He was looking into my eyes now, but the old, burning look of love had been replaced by cold contempt. I shivered inside. I felt dead. "Oh? And who were these so-called friends?" I asked, my voice a dry whisper.

"One of them was called Lori. Short brown hair, goes out with a guy called Carl. His father's a business acquaintance of my dad's. The other was a pretty girl, with dark, curly hair and huge eyes. Rosie, I think she was called."

Pretty? Rosie Francks? Was that how boys saw

her? Lori and I had always thought she was really ugly.

Steeling myself to look Gary in the eye and knowing that the future of our love affair depended entirely on what I was about to say, and whether he believed me or not, I said, "Gary, I want to tell you about Sim and what happened to me after. Please listen."

And I told him about how I'd vowed I'd never sleep with a boy until I was in love, and how I'd imagined I was in love with Sim, and how I'd found out he was cheating on me and had felt so let down and desperate that I'd thrown myself at two other boys, just to try and get over Sim.

"It wasn't half the boys at my school! It was just three – " Gosh, that sounded dreadful! – "and it was all a big mistake, I know that now. But those girls hate me and when they found out about it, they started the 'slag' campaign. It was really cruel and unfair. Everyone knows Rosie and Shaz sleep around, but nobody calls them slags because they wouldn't dare.

"You've no idea what I went through before I met you, Gary. And then, when we fell in love, I was so happy. At last I knew what love really felt like."

I gazed pleadingly at him, willing him to forgive me. I searched his face for signs of his expression softening, a smile beginning, his eyes losing their hard, bleak, accusing look.

He stood up and my heart missed a beat.

"Sorry, Rachel, but I think this is over," he said, and then he walked out on me. Just walked out, without even saying goodbye.

The days that followed were far and away the worst ones of my life – worse even than the days of the "slag" business.

Mary and Kirsty were really kind. "Come over, we'll cheer you up," they kept inviting me. I went once, but I was such bad company that I apologized for myself and went home early. I couldn't have a giggle and a good, girlie time. I didn't have it in me. But they kept on ringing and even came round once and dragged me out to the park. They chatted while I tagged silently along like a wet week – or rather, a sopping wet century. It may have been sunny outdoors, but I was raining inside, a positive monsoon!

Whatever anyone said to try and cheer me up, there was no one else I wanted in the whole wide world but Gary.

It was several days before I could get hold of Carol-Ann, but when she heard my tale of woe at last, she insisted that I come and stay with her as soon as possible. She and Joel were going away a few days later, but she said I could stay on and have their room if I liked. She even offered to lend me some money.

Just before I went, a package arrived for me. When I opened it, I found that it contained the gold chain I'd bought for Gary. I stared at it, feeling really sick. I didn't need it now – didn't want it. And I certainly couldn't pay for it because I'd done nothing about finding a job. There was only one thing for it: I had to sit down and write a letter saying that the chain was no longer required, and wrap it up and send it back, hoping they'd accept it and not give me any trouble.

When I got back from Carol-Ann's, though, my heart sank in dread because that familiar looking package was back. The company had enclosed a letter saying that, as nothing was wrong with the product itself, they couldn't take it back and I was committed to paying for it. It was a nightmare. I would just have to ask Mum to lend me some money.

Or maybe I could ask Ollie. He had a good job now. I'd paid him a visit in London and was amazed to find that his room in the house he shared was neat and tidy and – even more of a miracle – that he'd given up smoking. He was even planning to buy his own small flat. He was a reformed character. If he lent me fifty pounds and Pete lent me fifty, I'd be OK.

Slightly cheered by this hope, I turned my mind to wondering what to do with the chain. Then it came to me. I could still send it to Gary. Perhaps it would make him change his mind. I still couldn't believe that, after all the wonderful times we'd shared, and the sheer bliss of our lovemaking, he could drop me just like that, especially after I'd told him the truth.

Maybe he didn't like the fact that I'd slept with other guys before him. That was crazy, though. As he got older and met women who were in their twenties, he couldn't expect them not to have a past. Everybody had one.

I told him that, in the note I wrote to accompany the chain.

Dearest Gary, I wrote.

I'm missing you so much. Please believe that I never lied to you. You never asked if I was a virgin. If you had done, I would have told you I wasn't. What does it matter, anyway? Everyone has a past of some sort, even you, though you've never told me about it. It's what's inside a person's heart that matters, not things they've done before they met you. I happen to love you very much and I'd never do a thing to hurt you. I'm not a slag and I've never been one, and since

I met you I've had nothing to do with any other boy.

I bought you this chain just before we split up. I was going to give it to you as a present, as a token of my feelings for you. I still want you to have it. And please, please, let's talk about all this. I can't bear this silence, it's killing me.

All my love, Rachel.

I knew that the end sounded a bit dramatic, but it was honestly how I felt. Not seeing him – not even getting any phone calls from him – *was* killing me.

Three days after sending Gary the chain, I got it back by Recorded Delivery. My eyes blurred with tears, I struggled to open it and see what he'd written inside. But there was nothing except the chain; no note, nothing.

That night, Mum went out and I started reading her magazines to distract myself. In one of the agony columns was a letter from someone who, like me, was heartbroken after a breakup with her boyfriend. The agony aunt said that the first few weeks would be the worst and that she should try and fill her time up with lots of distractions, so she wouldn't be able to think about him all the time.

To me, it was like a message from my

guardian angel. I needed a distraction that would last all day and what could be better than a job, which my finances really needed? Next day I went out job-hunting and, to my surprise, landed one almost instantly in a big DIY super-store who'd advertised for staff in the local paper.

For two weeks, I was thoroughly distracted as I learned the ropes and settled in to the routine of working. Then it all fell apart again. As I picked up my diary to write in it one night, it happened to fall open at a date with a ring round it. The date of my last period. I hadn't had one since.

With trembling fingers, I thumbed through the pages, my brain madly counting. I did it twice, three times, but there seemed no doubt about it: I was a week overdue!

Chapter 15

My stomach churned and I felt terribly sick. Was it morning sickness or just the shock of my discovery? I ran to the bathroom but nothing happened, so I went back to my bedroom and sat on the edge of the bed, feeling faint.

I thought back to the day Gary and I had made love. Icy dread clawed at my guts. It had to have happened then – and I thought we'd been so careful. . .

Carol-Ann! I had to ring her. She'd know what to do. I was about to go and get the phone when I remembered that she and Joel had gone away to Portugal and wouldn't be back yet. They were staying in a villa owned by friends of Joel's. It was a holiday of a lifetime for her and an utter disaster for me. Who could I run to with my problems now?

I threw myself face down on the pillow and sobbed my heart out, but unfortunately the pillow didn't smother the sounds of my misery completely enough, because a few minutes later I heard a knock at my door and Mum's voice calling anxiously, "Rachel? Rachel, are you all right in there?"

"Go away!" I yelled, but the next moment she'd come in.

"Sweetheart, what's wrong?" she asked.

"Oh, nothing. Just Gary, that's all. I . . . I miss him so much!"

"Never mind, love, you'll soon get over him. It'll just take a bit of time, that's all," she said soothingly.

It was all very well for her to talk, I thought bitterly. She had Ken. Perhaps they'd get married. I wouldn't even be able to be a bridesmaid if I was pregnant.

Mum offered to make us both a cup of tea and went downstairs. I dried my eyes and splashed my face with cold water in the bathroom. As I blinked and mopped my face dry with the towel, I thought that a few more days weren't going to make any difference. Carol-Ann would be back next Sunday and I'd ask her then. In the meantime, I confided in my two best friends, Mary and Kirsty, who did their best to comfort me.

"I read an article which said that if you get really upset, it can mess up your cycle," Kirsty said.

"You've had school exams, plus breaking up with Gary. I should think that's enough to do it," Mary pointed out. "You're only a bit overdue, I don't think you should panic yet. My periods are often late."

"I hope you're right," I said gloomily. When Carol-Ann got back, her first words were pretty similar to Mary's. She, too, said I shouldn't panic. Apparently, she'd had pregnancy scares too, and every time it had all turned out OK. It was just her periods being irregular. Her second piece of advice was to buy a pregnancy testing kit.

"But I can't! They all know me at the chemist's. They'd say something to Mum!" I exclaimed fearfully.

"Then go to another chemist, dummy! Try Boots in the High Street. They'll have them there. Follow the instructions very carefully – I've messed up a few in my time because I didn't do it right. Ring me the moment you get the result. Promise? Do it tomorrow. I'll be in all day, just waiting."

I promised. She was such a great support to

me. I don't know what I'd have done without her.

Next day, I went out in my lunch hour and bought one of the kits, surprised at how many different ones there were. I asked which was the easiest to use and the assistant suggested one. When I got home, I took it out of my shoulder-bag. The paper bag rustled in my hand as I stared at it. Did I honestly have the courage to go through with this?

That night I lay awake for ages. It was gone three in the morning before I plucked up the courage to carry out the test. Keeping my ears strained for the faintest sound, I crept into the bathroom and followed the instructions on the packet.

"Please, *please*, God, don't let me be pregnant!" I prayed. "I'll give up boys for ever. I'll even become a nun. Just don't let me be pregnant!"

I read the leaflet. There were two windows on the plastic wand. If the big window stayed white, I wasn't pregnant, but if it went blue. . .

I held the wand under the light and let out my breath in a gusty sigh. It was colourless. I was all right! I started to dance around the room. Then, through the wall, I heard Mum cough. Oh, no! I thought. What if she comes in the bathroom before I've had a chance to hide all the evidence?

I bundled everything up in a towel and took it into my bedroom, where I transferred it all to a plastic bag and shoved it into my shoulderbag for disposal the following day. Only then, at almost half-past four, did I go to bed, but I didn't care how tired I was going to feel next day because the miracle I'd prayed for had been granted me. I wasn't pregnant after all!

Next day, I couldn't wait to ring my sister, who was as delighted as I was. Then I rang Kirsty. She and Mary were going shopping and asked if I'd like to join them. It was just what I needed.

I told them about my negative pregnancy test and they were thrilled. They said they'd been really worried for me.

We shopped all morning. I couldn't afford to buy anything because of paying the instalments on the gold chain, but Mary bought some shoes and Kirsty bought a dress.

We went to a burger bar for lunch. We were chatting quite normally, when Mary suddenly shocked me by saying, "I saw Gary down town the other day. He was coming out of the bookshop."

My immediate question was, "Was he with anyone?"

She smiled reassuringly. "No, he was on his own."

Although it didn't prove anything, I instantly felt better. "Are you going to wear that dress for the party?" I asked Kirsty, meaning my brother Pete's twenty-first in two weeks' time.

"I might do," she said. After that, all we talked about was what we were going to wear and who might be coming. There was one person I knew for sure *wouldn't* be coming, and that was the one person I longed to see. . .

The day after our shopping expedition, my long-awaited period started. Even though I got the normal pains and spots, I was over the moon! It looked as if the theory about anxiety stopping periods could have been right.

Whatever, I didn't care. I was OK. Except I wasn't, because I didn't have Gary, and with every day that passed, I missed him more.

I wondered about him constantly. Did he ever miss me? Was he happy? Had he found a holiday job? He'd said something about his father finding him something, but his dad was hardly ever around as he spent most of his time in London, so how could he? Unless he had contacts among local businessmen. . .

I'd probably never know, so I pushed it right out of my mind and devoted myself instead to helping Mum organize Pete's twenty-first.

* * *

174

Carol-Ann and Ollie had promised to come up from London for the party. I couldn't wait to see my sister and I surprised myself by finding I wanted to see Ollie again, too.

We were having it at home because it was cheaper. Pete was bringing loads of friends from the gym. Some of them were bound to be hunky fellas, but nobody would ever be a patch on Gary.

I fully intended to play barmaid or dee-jay, so I could lurk in a corner or behind a table all evening, because I certainly wasn't feeling very sociable. We were going to have a barbecue so everyone would be outside if the weather was good. Even if it wasn't, the food would be cooked on the barbie. Fortunately, the twins were going to their grandparents' for the week-end, so there would be no tiny burned fingers.

As the day approached, I made my own preparations. I bought a huge card with a picture of the Chippendales on it and wrote inside: *To my brother, who's hunkier than any of them, and much, much brighter.* Well, none of them were going to read it, were they? I'd had a T-shirt made with his picture on the front — the shop had done it from a photo I'd taken in. It looked really good. I enclosed a note saying that as soon as I had more money, I'd buy him something extra to go with it.

Carol-Ann and Joel arrived the night before. It was fantastic to have my sister back home. We hugged and clung to one another. She told me I looked amazingly well despite all my problems, which gave my ego a boost.

Ollie arrived on the Saturday morning. He was going to doss in Pete's room with him, as his old one was needed for the party. It was to be the dancing room, and the lounge would be for people who wanted to sit down. Coats and bags were to be left in my room. I didn't mind. I was sure I wouldn't want to go to bed early.

At last guests started to arrive. Ollie had volunteered to do the cooking, so I took turns with Mum at being "greeter".

By ten-thirty, the party was in full swing and Kirsty and Mary were being chatted up by two of Ollie's friends – not the dreadful John, thank God! He hadn't been invited, on my strict orders.

Pete said there were some people still to come, who had had to work late. Around eleven, the doorbell rang and I went to let them in. A bloke and two girls walked in. I recognized both girls because they worked in Reception at the gym. The guy was Craig, an old school friend of Pete's. It was Craig who'd got Pete the interview at the gym which had led to the job.

"Hi, Craig! I think there's still some food left. Hi, Sophie! Hi, Kate!" I said.

Then a second bloke stepped out of the shadows, a dazzlingly handsome one in a snow-white shirt and black jeans, the street lights gleaming on his jet black hair.

"Are you going to say 'hi' to me, too, or aren't I welcome?" Gary asked softly.

Chapter 16

When I didn't answer immediately, he made as if to turn away.

"No, no – don't go," I said weakly, feeling so dizzy that I had to hang on to the door-frame.

He stopped and looked at me slightly sheepishly.

"What are you doing here?" I asked him.

"Your brother invited me. I'm working behind the bar at the gym."

I hadn't been there for weeks, because of work and lack of money.

"He didn't tell me you were working there," I said.

"I asked him not to," Gary explained. He had a tan. He looked fantastic.

"Oh." It was a blow. He obviously hadn't

wanted anything to do with me. I looked down at my feet.

"Maybe I'd better go, then," he said. "Give this to Pete for me, would you?"

He handed me a gift-wrapped bottle, probably something expensive that should be kept away from the party guests. I held my hand out for it, then withdrew it.

"I think you should give it to him yourself," I said, holding the door open for him.

My heart was hammering so hard that I could hardly breathe as Gary brushed past me in the doorway.

"Everyone's in the garden," I said.

"In that case. . ." Gary paused at the door of the lounge. "Can I talk to you for a moment?"

In a split second, a dozen different scenarios flickered through my mind but, as it turned out, none of them was the right one. For, the moment I followed him into the empty lounge, he took me in his arms.

His lips searched mine with a hungry passion and I found myself mumbling, "Oh Gary, Gary!" as tears welled up in my eyes.

"Ssh, there!" he murmured, brushing my hair soothingly with his hand. "I've missed you, too."

"You *have*?" I couldn't believe it. "I thought you hated me. . . You thought I was a slag. . ."

"Sit down." He pulled me on to the sofa beside him. "I've been doing a lot of thinking," he said. "We can all get things wrong sometimes. Perhaps I was wrong about you."

I raised my eyebrows enquiringly and waited for him to continue. He took my left hand, held it between his hands and stroked it gently, a touch which sent little rippling thrills right through me.

"I've talked to your brother," he said.

"What? Pete? He doesn't know anything about me!" I protested.

"You'd be surprised!" Gary gave a gentle laugh. "He told me you'd never really had a boyfriend before Sim, and that he'd two-timed you and broken your heart, and then you'd gone out with a couple more boys on the rebound and someone had stirred things at school and called you all kinds of things that weren't true.

"It all matched what you'd said, Rachel. You were brave enough to tell me all about your past, but I didn't want to hear it. I'm sorry. Call it hurt pride, if you like. I didn't like to think you might have slept with blokes who were better at it than me!"

His eyes met mine in an honest, open, apologetic look. "I want to tell you something about me now," he said. "I'm not that experienced, Rachel, but I've had a past, too. I had a girlfriend called Angela and we slept together several times. And before her, there was this girl who lived near me who slept with anything in trousers. I'm ashamed to say I was one of them. That was my first time and it was horrible!

"But that time with you was something really special for me. Was it for you, too?"

My eyes filled up with tears, which spilled down my cheeks. I felt I was looking at him through vast lakes as I said, "Of course it was. It felt like the first time ever. I loved you so much!"

"*Loved?* Past tense? Does that mean you don't care any more?"

Those sky-coloured eyes of his were searing into mine like blue flames, making me nervous so that I said all the wrong things.

"No – I mean, yes. I do care. Very much. I've thought about you all the time, every day. I was so upset, I couldn't bear it!"

He squeezed my hand, then pulled me towards him and kissed me, the light kiss of a friend at first, which then strengthened into the more powerful one of a lover.

"Do you – could you . . . still love me?" he asked, when he'd stopped kissing me.

Through my tears, I gave an incredulous laugh. "Love you? I've never stopped loving you. Of course I still love you!" I blurted out.

He kissed my forehead, both cheeks, then the end of my nose. "There's a tear on your nose," he said, and brushed it off with his finger.

"What do you say to us forgetting the past and making a new start? No Sim or the others, no Angela or that other girl, just us two, as if we'd never known anybody else?" he said.

"Oh yes, *please*!" I said eagerly.

"I've brought you something," he said, fishing in his pocket. He pulled out a small gold packet and handed it to me. Inside, nestling in crimson tissue paper, were two beautiful silver earrings in the shape of fishes.

I gasped. "They're lovely!" I said, taking off the ones I was wearing and putting the fishes on instead.

Suddenly, I remembered the gold chain. Surely Gary wouldn't reject it a second time?

"Hang on a minute," I told him, and dashed upstairs.

I came down with the box hidden behind my back.

"Gary, I sent you a present, remember? You sent it back. Well, I hope you'll accept it now."

"I don't deserve it," he said as I handed him the box. "I'll only accept it if it's for the next two Christmases and birthdays combined!"

"Do you think we might be going out that

long?" I said lightly, my heart hammering.

"I hope so," he answered.

I couldn't speak, but I gave him a look which I hoped conveyed all the love I felt for him. It must have worked because, without any more objection, he unfastened the clasp and put the chain on.

"How does it look?" he asked, undoing another button of his white shirt.

The effect was just what I'd dreamed of, only better, the thin gold gleaming against his tan.

"It looks gorgeous," I assured him, kissing his throat, in the hollow above his collarbone.

"Ooh, that tickles!" he said. "Come here and let me thank you properly!"

It was a long time later that we joined the party. People were starting to go home, but, for me, the night – and the rest of my life – were just beginning.

Look out for other Confessions in this revealing series.

"My boyfriend's older than my dad"

"But they've got to let you go some day," James argued. "You can't stay Daddy's little girl for ever. What are you now – twenty-two, twenty-three? You're not a kid any more, Natasha!"

There was an awful silence.

Oh God! I thought, he really doesn't know how old I am.

"Natasha?"

"Yes?"

I was thinking furiously. Should I tell him? Should I? I thought of all the trouble my last little white lie had got me into, with Mum and Dad. I hadn't meant any harm, but still, a lie was a lie. I wanted to have an honest relationship with James. No secrets. The sort of relationship where we could trust each other, tell each other the truth about anything and everything.

"Is something the matter?"

I managed to smile. "No, not really," I said, my heart thumping. "It's just that I – er . . . you seem to think I'm a bit older than I really am, James."

"Older?" James echoed.

"Yes. I only left school this summer, after A levels."

James nearly choked on his pint. Then he looked at me with an expression of such horror on his face that I didn't know whether to laugh or cry.

"You've only just left school?" he repeated.

"In July. After A levels."

Cold fingers of fear clutched at my heart. Surely it didn't matter that much how old I was? But it seemed as though it did.

"Natasha," James said, in a totally expressionless voice, "how old are you?"

"I was eighteen on August 3rd," I said, really frightened now.

James didn't say anything.

"But – but why?" I asked him. "Does it matter? James?" I caught hold of the sleeve of his jacket. Slowly, he rubbed his hands over his face, then turned to look at me.

"Darling," he said, "do you know how old I am?"

"Well, no," I stammered, "not exactly. I mean, you're working and everything. I thought you were – I don't know – twenty-seven, twenty-eight? About that, anyway."

"Twenty-eight!" said James flatly.

"Why?" I faltered. "How old are you?"

"I'm thirty-six," he said.

"*Thirty-six?*" I gasped. "But – but that's—"

"That's what?"

I just couldn't take it in. James was thirty-six! My dad was only thirty-five; he and Mum had both been seventeen when I was born.

"My dad's younger than you are!" I whispered.

I was in a state of total shock. It was as though someone had emptied a bucket of ice-cold water over me. My lovely new boyfriend was *older than my dad*!

"Natasha, I'm – I'm sorry," said James, taking my hand in his. I couldn't even look at him.

"Sorry?" I said roughly. "What d'you mean, sorry? You've – you've got nothing to be sorry for. You can't help being – " I sniffed – "thirty-six, any more than I can help being eighteen!"

James heaved a huge sigh. "I'm twice your age," he said hopelessly. "It's not right."

I stared at him in panic. "Not right?" I said. "What d'you mean, not right?"

Surely, *surely* he wasn't going to finish it? Finish everything, after all he'd said. . .

"I'm too old for you," said James gently, "that's all there is to it. Natasha, you're a lovely girl. You've got all your life ahead of you. You should be with someone your own age, some young lad who'll give you a good time, do all the things you want to do, not some old has-been like me."

"I – I – " I stammered, "it's not *like* that, James! I don't want someone my own age. Truly I don't. Boys of eighteen are just that – boys. Dean, my ex-boyfriend, was just a kid, going on half the time about football and how drunk he and the lads got last time they went out. That's all so childish, and it's not what I want. And – and the other night, some guy in the pub tried to chat me up and I – I just wasn't interested. It's you I want to be with, James, honestly. I don't care how old you are."

"Yes, you do," said James. "You looked horrified just now, when I told you I was thirty-six."

"It was a shock," I admitted. "I told you, I thought you were in your late twenties." But I love you, anyway, I said silently to myself. That's what really matters.

"Besides," James was saying, "what on earth are your family going to think?"

I shook my head. I might pretend to myself that it didn't matter what Mum and Dad thought, but I knew it did. Dad was already touchy about James. If I let slip that James was actually thirty-six, he'd go spare!

Point Romance

Are you burning with passion, and aching with desire? Then these are the books for you! Point Romance brings you passion, romance, heartache ... and *love*.